THE NERDY DOZEN

CLOSE ENCOUNTERS
OF THE NERD KIND

JEFF MILLER

THE NERDY DOZEN

CLOSE ENCOUNTERS OF THE NERD KIND

HARPER

An Imprint of HarperCollins*Publishers*

alloy**entertainment**

Produced by Alloy Entertainment
1700 Broadway, New York, NY 10019

Design by Liz Dresner

Library of Congress Control Number: 2014958871
ISBN 978-0-06-227265-2

15 16 17 18 19   CG/RRDH   10 9 8 7 6 5 4 3 2 1
❖
First Edition

Per Ardua ad Astra

For Zach

THE NERDY DOZEN

CLOSE ENCOUNTERS
OF THE NERD KIND

CHAPTER

1

STANDING IN A BEAM OF LIGHT, NEIL ANDERTOL GAZED AT A crisp American flag and a medal hanging from a silken cord. The award was a lustrous silver, and the word *HONOR* sat above three eagles.

Neil looked at his chest and could almost feel the heft of the medal as it rested above his heart. He closed his eyes and exhaled slowly. The days of keeping his military exploits a secret would soon be over. Eager to receive the military's highest honors, he stepped forward.

Smack.

"Ow!" Neil winced as he slammed his glasses into a Plexiglas case. He rubbed the grease smudge his nose left behind.

The showcase in front of Neil was filled with uniforms, honors, and a list of the dangerous, declassified missions completed by the American Air Force. Neil pictured himself in one of the flight jumpsuits—they looked exactly like the one Neil had worn when he piloted top secret technology over his Memorial Day long weekend.

Today, Neil's uniform was a gray hooded sweatshirt and wrinkled khaki shorts that had gone unwashed for the entire summer and into the second week of eighth grade at Romare Smythe Junior High. His black hair was shaggy, making him look younger, but also adding an extra inch to his height.

"What's that medal?" said Neil's friend Tyler, who was standing next to Neil and eating a piece of expired beef jerky.

With his pale skin and sunken eyes from late-night gaming sessions, Tyler looked like a cave creature—or, at least, an animal that a cave creature had captured to eat at a later time.

"Oh, nothing important," Neil replied. "What's the status of the mission?"

With a sideways glance at the nearby security guard, Tyler whispered, "I have acquired the wireless password." He crumpled his jerky wrapper and tossed it toward a trash can. He missed and went to go pick it up. "And I ran a test video—seven minutes should be no problem. The audio sounds great. We can do this."

"Copy that."

The two ran to catch up to their group, a pack of disinterested teenagers, also known as the annual eighth-grade field trip. Neil and his classmates were chaperoned by the gym teacher and wrestling coach, Mr. Rhome.

He was a stocky former semipro baseball player with scruffy hair and a duck-like waddle. To make matters worse, Mr. Rhome's favorite student was the bully Tommy Scott, who was leading the group with his cronies.

The field trip pushed on through the building's main corridor. A series of arched doorways led to the planetarium.

"Welcome to your own Greater Colorado Museum and Planetarium," a voice resonated from a speaker. The woman's voice was robotic, like a spaceship's evil artificial intelligence. "The next planetarium show will begin in thirteen minutes and forty-eight seconds."

"Perfect. Just enough time for a new record," Tyler said, rubbing his nose with the corner of his vest. He seemed to have an "anything goes" policy in terms of personal hygiene, always aggressively blowing his nose or clipping his fingernails in public places. Coming from a household where hands were sanitized roughly every twenty minutes, Neil was always a bit jealous.

"If we break the record, we'll definitely be in the 'Reboot Spotlight,'" Neil said excitedly.

The current online fad, "Guerilla IMAXing," involved playing the most difficult level of your favorite game projected in random public spaces. Games were broadcast on movie theater screens, sides of digital bus advertisements, or anywhere else creative nerds could think of. Neil had watched every video uploaded to his favorite gaming site, Internet Piraseas. From an online server aboard his private yacht, the site was run by Reboot Robiski, child hacker and international man of mystery. Videos in the "Reboot Spotlight" received instant fame.

Out of every available online clip, the only one attempted at a planetarium was a measly six minutes, with terrible quality and no audio. A few days before the field trip, Neil had recruited Tyler to help him pull off something much better.

Neil knew their mission would catch the eye of random gamers, but he couldn't help but think it would also impress his friends from the Chameleon Mission. He missed all of them, even Trevor at this point.

"Great job, Lieutenant," said Neil.

"You too, Viceroy," replied Tyler, who was still grasping the proper rank terminology.

Mr. Rhome slowed to a halt in the central hub of the Greater Colorado Museum and Planetarium *and* Homestyle Buffet. It was only recently that the all-you-can-eat buffet had been installed, hoping people would come for the food and stay for the exhibits. Sadly, it only proved that mini corn dogs were more popular than the sum of all human knowledge.

Neil watched the bustling entrance of the buffet, where children and their grandmothers in sparkly sweaters scurried to grab lunch.

"Okay, everyone! Here's the game plan: You all have tickets for the planetarium show in about thirteen minutes, after which you'll have a little time to explore the exhibits," said Mr. Rhome, handing a stack of tickets to the group.

"I'll meet you back at this spot in two hours," he went on. "I'd go with you, but it's a full house. Plus I hear this place has endless chicken tenders." The haggard gym teacher looked down at his watch and added, "Matter of fact, let's call it two and a half hours. Think I saw a soft-serve ice cream machine, too."

Neil watched his chaperone head off toward the famed one-hundred-foot-long salad bar. He'd worried that ditching the field trip would prove difficult, but Mr. Rhome obviously wanted the mission to succeed as well.

"And the vulture is out of the nest," whispered Neil to Tyler.

As Tommy Scott and other classmates began looking at a display on Siberian glaciers, Neil and Tyler sidled toward the planetarium. They had ten minutes and thirty-seven seconds to complete their Guerilla IMAXing before the show began. Time was of the essence.

The boys ducked under the velvet ropes at the entrance of a dark tunnel.

"Mission: Guerilla IMAX is fully a go," Neil said as

he and Tyler poked their heads in the empty planetarium. "And we've got the place to ourselves."

Tyler ran to the planetarium's massive projector and began connecting software. The start-up screen washed over the domed ceiling above them. Neil removed his gaming tablet from a baggy cargo pocket and powered it up.

It all reminded Neil of his mission from the beginning of the summer: the rush of danger, the buzz of the equipment in his hand. Playing games at home didn't give him the same sort of adrenaline—Neil needed more.

"Wanna come over tonight and do some gaming?" Tyler asked as he looked through the inside of his vest, which was lined with rows of cables and electronic adaptors. "My babysitter's pretty cool about curfews. We can stay up all night and play Enchanted Poachers. You can even roll the die first."

"Ah, thanks, Tyler," Neil said reluctantly. "But I've got a big team game of—"

"Oh, that's right, Chameleon. I forgot your big match was *this* Friday. Man, you really love this game," Tyler said. "Well, maybe I can give it another shot? Or just watch you, really. You're like a video game sensei."

"Um, well, tonight will be rough. Since I've refused to mow the lawn all summer out of protest, my mom's not really letting me have anybody over," Neil lied. "But Janey's doing karate tournaments all over the place these days, so some weekend I'll plan to stay with you." Neil tried to sound reassuring.

The truth was, Neil's mom probably wouldn't mind Tyler coming over. But Neil just couldn't risk him being around for the evening.

"I get it, no worries," said Tyler, his tongue darting at the corner of his mouth as he successfully logged onto the museum's system.

"Next time," Neil said, handing Tyler his gaming tablet to get set up. "I promise."

Every weekend since the Air Force had recruited him to rescue a top secret fighter jet, Neil tried to organize a huge game of Chameleon for all his fellow recruits. But whether it was Biggs moving his compost pile or Yuri's boarding school banning the internet, something always prevented the whole group from playing together. Sam was barely around, seemingly always swept along wherever her father was deployed. She was hardly ever logged on to Chameleon.

The game tonight was to be different, though. Neil had heard back from everyone, and all eleven had confirmed they'd make it. He was counting down the hours.

"Okay, we're set up," Tyler said, handing Neil's tablet back to him. He had a similar one cradled in his skinny hands. "I connected you wirelessly, and I'm plugged in to record. I'll get a screen capture of what's on the projector, and I'll time it as well. And I've piped in the audio to the speakers. This is gonna be unreal."

"You're getting a promotion, soldier," Neil said, excitement and nervousness competing for first place in the pit of his stomach.

Neil took a deep breath and lay down in a chair looking up. With shaky fingers, he pushed start, and Chameleon appeared overhead, projected out into the dome of the planetarium. It looked a little distorted at first, but Neil's eyes quickly adjusted. It was almost like watching a kaleidoscope.

"Awesome," Neil and Tyler said in unison as Neil's jet fighter appeared overhead. It sped ahead and executed a series of controlled rolls, the audio piping into the theater with crystal clear surround sound. A summer of playing Chameleon had Neil's skills in peak condition—not to mention, of course, that he had flown the real thing, a jet that actually turned invisible. As Neil executed flawless dives and took out countless enemy fighters, he lost sight of the fact that he was playing in a planetarium, completely illegally. He felt like he was back on the mission—back with his friends.

"We've passed seven minutes. The record is ours!" Tyler shouted, before quickly covering his mouth with a clammy hand.

Neil smiled, but heard a rustling from the doorway—the sound of the velvet ropes out front being unclipped.

"The vulture is coming back to the nest!" Tyler whispered. But Neil pressed on, knowing each passing second could lead to online celebrity. His palms grew sweaty, and he soon heard Tyler clanging around somewhere inside the projector. Neil turned his eyes from the planetarium's ceiling to the small screen of his tablet. He pressed a flurry of buttons, and his fighter was soon invisible. Neil tried to remember the subtle buzzing he felt when doing so in a real-life Chameleon.

But Neil's heart jumped as he heard a voice that was distinctly not Tyler's. Time was up.

A thin museum worker was leading the rest of Neil's class inside, ushering them into the open planetarium with a raised hand.

"Hello, everyone. My name is Nebula, and I'm an *extremely* unpaid volunteer at your favorite museum, planetarium, and buffet," said a girl who could've passed for Biggs's sister. She had chin-length brown hair that was clumped in dreadlocks and tied back. Over a long flowing skirt, she wore a blue polo with the museum's logo on it and a large round button that said ASK ME ABOUT OUR WALKING SUNDAE BAR TOUR!

"Oh, and nice to see a few of you already enjoying the facility," she said, looking at Neil and Tyler. Neil panicked and looked upward but was impressed to see only stars. Tyler had managed to switch the source on the fancy projector with only a second to spare. As if they were just waiting patiently, the two waved awkwardly from the cushy reclined seats adjacent to the projector.

Mission: Guerilla IMAX was a total success!

"Our state-of-the-art telescope is one of the largest in the West—able to see galaxies unfathomable distances away," Nebula explained. "Okay, everybody, time for the show!" she announced, drawing closed a heavy, light-blocking curtain in front of the planetarium's doorway. "I hope everyone has their exploring caps on. I know I do. I made it myself," said Nebula, who clearly wasn't wearing any type of visible real-world headwear.

Neil was impressed Tyler was miraculously able to change the video feed to the projector, and he slyly exited the game on his tablet before any noises gave him away. He breathed a sigh of relief. He'd done it.

"Hey, Night Light, don't get scared when it gets dark in here," yelled Tommy, biting into a vanilla ice cream cone despite the NO FOOD ALLOWED IN THE PLANETARIUM sign on the wall. "You can sit near an exit sign if you need the light."

After Neil beat Tommy at Chameleon—at Tommy's own sleepover—the bully's hatred of Neil had only gotten worse. He'd stopped calling Neil "Neandertol," but now he had a new nickname. While Neil had really left the sleepover to go help the Air Force, Tommy told everyone that Neil was too scared to stay over because he was afraid of the dark. And so "Night Light" was born.

As a promise to Major Jones, Neil made sure his adventure remained a secret, but it wasn't easy when he kept finding Disney princess lights plastered to his locker.

Nebula dimmed the lights, and the giant ceiling was illuminated with stars.

"Class, above you'll see the night sky as viewed through our telescope," Nebula said. "You can see how much more of the cosmos is visible without light pollution."

Neil watched as a comet or asteroid passed above. It cut through the sky in a bright slash.

"Was that an asteroid?" questioned Tyler.

"It could be," replied Nebula. "An asteroid last hit Earth sixty-six million years ago, and many scientists believe a crater in Mexico, just off the coast, is the mark of this impact. It wiped out any dinosaurs that were unable to fly," answered Nebula.

I wonder if Sam's heard of that crater. I'm sure she has. . . .

Neil missed talking with Sam daily and hearing her spout off all the random space knowledge bouncing around her brain.

"What's the crater called?" Neil asked.

"Will it happen again?" asked someone in a comfy chair behind Neil.

"Are you stupid? Of course it can't ever happen again. We'd blow it up before it even gets close," said Tommy.

"Chicxulub. The Chicxulub crater," said Nebula. "Something you can Google tonight after you plant the sapling I'm giving each of you."

Chicxulub. I'll tell Sam.

Just then a phone ring echoed through the expansive planetarium. Neil froze as he recognized the ringtone that continued to pulse—the one specifically designated for his mother.

Neil realized that while they successfully switched the video feed, he hadn't cut the audio from his game, and it was still being broadcast through the system's speakers. Tommy looked over and caught Neil squirming.

"Hm, well, can't say I've seen this before. If I could have everyone silence their phones, please," Nebula shouted over the phone ringing. After four beats Neil's phone once again went silent.

But before Neil could silence his phone, a bubbling sound alerted everyone in the planetarium that Neil had a new text. Tommy Scott cracked a devilish smile.

"Phone, read text," Tommy shouted right at Neil, using Neil's voice commands for evil purposes.

Oh no.

"Ah, ixnay that, phone robot."

"Reading text from Mom," a choppy robot voice said over the speakers. "Hey, Neil."

Tommy Scott turned to Neil with a smug smile.

"Janey's waiting to hear about being an alternate for a big karate tournament this weekend. Just wanted to keep you updated. Love you, Boogercheeks. Mommy."

Neil wanted to melt into the slanted floor below him. Everyone around him laughed as Tommy Scott high-fived anyone in a four-foot radius.

"Folks, this behavior is strictly against museum policy," said Nebula through gritted teeth. "Who among you is Boogercheeks? Show yourself! The remainder of the show's been canceled. I'm finding your teacher."

Wishing he could just disappear, Neil strained his eyes upward toward the live feed of space. His focus was quickly drawn to a bright light. It looked like the asteroid they saw earlier, but it was moving faster and upward. It lingered in sight a bit longer, then sped off in a smooth crescent away from the range of the telescope.

"Hey, what was that flash of light that just happened? That seemed different from that asteroid," Neil asked Nebula as the houselights were turned back on.

"Probably just space junk, kid," Nebula snapped. "Now, all of you, head out!"

Neil rushed out of the planetarium before the rest of the class, heading toward the parking lot with their school's bus and past the buffet. He was nearly to a buffet station featuring large pieces of meat being hacked apart under warm lamps when he heard the dense, husky voice of one Tommy Scott.

"Way to go, Night Light," he shouted at Neil. "Now we have to go back to school. And we don't even get to eat."

Neil turned away and kept walking, toward what looked to be a dinosaur skeleton made out of rotini. But Tommy wouldn't be ignored as he reached for a fistful of applesauce and flung it at the back of Neil's neck. Neil's back arched from cold shock as the soppy fruit sauce dripped down his back.

"What are you gonna do about it, Night Light?" Tommy snorted.

Neil turned away to avoid anything further, but he felt a blob of pudding splatter on his back.

Okay, not cool.

Neil turned around, staring at Tommy Scott and the two lackeys positioned behind him.

"You know what, applesauce me once, shame on me. But do it twice, ham on you," Neil said, grabbing a few glistening chunks of carved ham. He tossed them perfectly at Tommy, connecting solidly with his face and chest. While it maybe wasn't his best pun, Neil felt pretty good about it. But after Tommy mopped the cooked meat from his face, the food fight was officially on.

He threw the face ham back at Neil, but it hit a group of kids having lunch with their babysitter. Neil turned to apologize but was greeted with a few handfuls of spaghetti.

"Food fight!" yelled Tyler, who rushed to Neil's side. He slung sliced beets like tiny Frisbees, while ladles full of mashed potatoes flew in all directions. Everyone in the general area, child or not, began firing back. Neil witnessed a full-grown man wearing a shirt with two wolves on it chuck spare ribs at a group of Neil's classmates. Cubes of Jell-O bounced across the floor as Tommy and a goon cranked on the soft-serve ice cream machine.

Tommy let frozen clumps fill his hand before catapulting them Neil's way. Neil grabbed a tray to use as a shield and did his best to deflect the rounds being fired at him. But as the food-launching chaos grew more intense, the ear-piercing shriek of Mr. Rhome's whistle caught everyone's attention. Neil was frozen in mid–Brussels sprout toss.

"Andertol! I can't believe you!" Mr. Rhome shouted, spitting out chicken nuggets. He stood next to Nebula and a middle-aged museum director with wispy black and gray hair. "Sounds like we're gonna have to cancel this trip and leave early because of you! And now this?"

The rest of Neil's classmates groaned as they brushed peas out of their hair.

Neil and Tommy glared at each other as they slowly dropped any edible weaponry.

"And you'll all figure out how to repay damages," said the museum worker next to Mr. Rhome. "You kids got vanilla soft-serve all over the Neanderthal exhibit. Those cavemen are dry-clean only!"

Neil felt one hundredth his normal size. He had gone from the highest heights of filmed online gaming immortality to the museum's number one public enemy, completely soaked in Thousand Island dressing.

CHAPTER 2

NEIL HOPPED DOWN THE STAIRS OF HIS SCHOOL BUS AND heard the doors squeak shut. The bus rumbled into gear and drove away in a black cloud of exhaust. From the corner of his eye, he watched a car slowly turn a corner and creep up behind him. Neil cocked his head to see a glossy black vehicle, and his pulse jumped in anticipation. For the last three months, any dark SUV had Neil hoping for another adventure, another burlap sack to be thrown over his head.

As Neil's neighbor rolled by with a cheery wave from

her decidedly not-undercover car, he knew it was an ordinary bad day.

I do have gravy still in my sock, so maybe not totally ordinary.

Sunshine peeked over the clouds as Neil followed the street to his house. On his porch, he grasped the front door's handle and pushed, but it was locked.

"Mom! Janey! Open up!" Neil yelled, ringing the doorbell. After a few more fist pounds and no response, Neil turned to the front yard. He grabbed the family's secret rock that housed a key and, currently, two slugs.

Neil pushed open the door and returned the house key to the fake rock.

"Hello? Anybody?" Neil asked to no response, stepping into the kitchen. "I also just want to get this out of the way, but there's a good chance I'm banned for life from the museum."

No one replied.

He saw a sticky note clinging to the hood above the stove, and Neil could hear his mother's hurried tone as she scribbled:

Hi, honey, Janey was accepted into the karate tournament I called you about—woo-hoo!

Neil shook his head and ate an angry bite of cereal, wondering if starting tomorrow he would be known as Boogercheeks to the entire eighth grade, and possibly ninth.

It's an hour north, so we had to get on the road. We'll be back Sunday, and Dad should be, too, but his site needed him to work through the weekend somewhere in Montana. The sitter should be there around five. Love you, Mom.

"A sitter? Aw, man," Neil said to the stove. That meant hanging out with a community college sophomore named Vanessa, who refused to let Neil play video games all night. She used phrases like "Your brain needs to be engaged" and "Video games rot your third eye." Neil despised Vanessa weekends, and he couldn't wait until he could stay at home alone. His mother always promised he could when he turned fourteen, and his winter birthday couldn't come soon enough.

"Skeeroonk!"

An animal squawk rang out from the backyard.

"Okay, okay, Regina," Neil said, shaking his head as he scurried toward the sound. He spilled out from the back door toward a small fenced-in area tucked between two seven-foot-tall hedges.

Neil squished through the foliage and opened a gate in the fence to reveal a tiny ostrich, complete with a full house and habitat. She was much shorter than the ones Neil had seen—and ridden—on his mission to a South Pacific island chain, because she was still young. She had arrived that summer as a large speckled egg, in a wooden crate from Harris. Neil took it as Harris's way of apologizing for the whole "stealing top secret intel to become the kingpin of the video game underworld" ordeal. Neil's mother and father took it as an attempt to kill all the grass on their lawn.

He had fibbed, telling them it was a class pet that grew too big for the classroom and that he had been selected as its lucky caretaker. Neil knew this would buy him enough time to figure out where he could house a fully grown ostrich.

"Hi, Regina," Neil said to the tiny animal. She cocked her head and pecked at the ground. "I'm not gonna reach my hand in there for a while. You almost took a pinkie off the other day. I've got a big match that's going to start soon."

Neil tossed two handfuls of Grade A ostrich pellets into Regina's cage and filled her water dish. She spread her wings and flapped them a couple times.

"See you later, Regina," he said, and he turned back to his house. He grabbed a juice from the kitchen and bounded up his carpeted stairs with a grin. He pressed a button on his white controller and jolted his console out of sleep mode. His in-box held a total of three new messages. Neil clicked on the first, an audio message from Sam. It was her first in weeks: "Going to get another practice session in with Fury, may be a bit late for the team game. Excited to play!"

Neil smiled. It was good to hear that familiar voice of Sam's. The very one Neil took to be a boy's for roughly a year.

He looked at a disc labeled SHUTTLE FURY and contemplated playing it. It was the game that NASA had sent to all the kids after the success of their first mission. But it just wasn't . . . fun.

Tomorrow, Neil said to himself, like he did every night.

It's not that he hadn't *tried* to beat it; he just got beyond frustrated with the space simulator. The clunky graphics looked at least ten years old, the ship itself didn't do any cool tricks, and the game itself was too hard—Neil never had trouble beating games after enough time, but he couldn't seem to figure out this one's secrets.

Neil grabbed the Shuttle Fury disc and sighed deeply before moving it toward his gaming console. He placed it on the end table next to his favorite comfy chair and perched his juice box on top.

At least the game works as a coaster.

With ten minutes until the big game, Neil opened his next unread message, a video from Biggs: "Hey, Neil! Sorry, but gonna have to bail on the game tonight. We'll play again soon, though," he said, nodding and smiling into the camera. "Just heard about a big lecture on carp destroying the ecosystem, and I can't miss it. This is my Christmas."

Neil shrugged his shoulders and laughed. While he was upset the big game would no longer happen with everyone, he couldn't stay mad. But as the minutes edged along toward game time, nobody else seemed to be logging on. Neil listened for the familiar notifications alerting him of his friends signing on, but he only heard the whirring fan inside his game console. Where was everybody?

The doorbell rang, echoing through the empty house. Neil sighed. His friends can't show up on time, but of course the babysitter is early.

He walked slowly to the front door, dragging his feet to savor his freedom, knowing he would soon be under the control of Vanessa.

He unlatched the dead bolt and pulled the door open.

"Hey, Vanessa," Neil mumbled, trying to turn back around and head upstairs quickly. He figured he could grab two days' worth of food and juice in his arms and lock himself in his room until Sunday, relieving himself out of an open window every few hours or so.

But when he heard the gravelly-sounding voice of a man, Neil turned back to face the doorway.

"You were expecting a babysitter, Andertol?" Major Jones said, spitting sunflower seed shells into Neil's front yard. "Come on. We need your help. Again."

CHAPTER

3

NEIL'S FINGERS TRACED THE STITCHING OF THE SAFETY harness locking him in place. It passed across both shoulders and latched into the stiff metal seat beneath his thin legs. Even after a summer growth spurt, his feet didn't quite touch the floor. He was alone in the belly of a huge cargo plane as Jones assisted with the landing in the cockpit.

As Neil stared down the row of empty seats, he plucked a piece of crouton from his hair. Before being whisked away by Jones, he'd used a wet kitchen towel to give himself a post-museum shower, but his hair was apparently saving some leftovers.

"Initiating final descent" came a voice through the headset hugging Neil's ears. The plane dropped, flipping Neil's stomach. He pinched his nose and popped his ears to equalize the change in pressure, something he'd picked up during the last mission. "Prepare for landing."

"If I had a tray table, it would be up," Neil shouted back over the engine noise.

Turbulence shook the plane violently, but Neil remained surprisingly calm. As the massive plane's landing gear made contact with the ground, he was focused on breathing.

Exhale . . . two . . . three . . . four.

It was advice he'd found online from a retired Air Force pilot, and one of many professional flying tips Neil was anxious to show off. He'd done some thorough Googling about real-life pilots, and was ready to prove he was one as well.

The internet stranger, going by the moniker the Invisible Coyote, said that pilots in tight formation would even learn to breathe at the same time. Neil and Biggs tried practicing in a game of Chameleon weeks before, but Neil accidentally hit the mute button and nearly suffocated his friend and fellow pilot.

"All right, Andertol. Let's move," said Jones, emerging from the cockpit.

The plane rolled to a stop, and Neil heard the rear hydraulic hatch engage and begin to open. Sunlight quickly filled the ship's cargo hold, casting a long shadow behind Jones's muscular frame.

"Sir, yes, sir, Major Jones," Neil replied with a nod. He removed his headset and freed himself from his seat's nylon safety web.

The camouflaged soldier didn't reply and stomped down the ship's metal hatch. Neil followed Jones out onto the runway, jittering with excitement and a completely full bladder. The sun was beginning to set behind a glob of cauliflower-shaped clouds, and the smell of salt water from a nearby ocean brushed past Neil's nose. Wherever he was, it was far from his landlocked home.

While a map or travel brochure on his current location would have been nice, he did appreciate the Air Force's "burlap bag–free" approach they must have recently adopted. A certain amount of trust could be earned when you weren't blindfolded in a trunk or backseat.

"So, what's the mission, Major?"

"First things first, Andertol—it's Major General Jones, now," the soldier shouted to Neil as they marched away from the roar of the cargo plane's engine.

"Oh, nice! A promotion," Neil gushed. They headed toward a tall, looming white building. "Do you get any fancy new pins or medals? Do they have a good jangle to them?"

Jones shook his head and patted Neil's back with a huge, rough hand. It knocked the gamer's bony body forward a few inches as they crossed over the still-warm asphalt. They neared the entrance of the giant structure, an obvious aircraft hangar of some kind.

"You know what? I think I've missed you, Andertol."

Neil smiled to himself with pride. Those weren't words he ever expected to hear from someone who seemed to always need a nap.

As the rickety metal doors of the hangar opened, the last of the day's sunshine spilled onto the interior of the hangar floor's taupe-colored concrete. The structure was vast and empty, like a hollowed-out steel turtle shell.

A gaggle of determined people in orange, blue, and

white jumpsuits scurried around the facility. A few furiously tapped on computers and handheld tablets, while others lugged hoses and electrical cords from one side of the building to the next. Their shoes were covered with white booties that kept subtly slipping on the slick floor. A gigantic American flag was hung on the wall opposite the only doors leading out, with smaller flags from other countries just below.

Neil scanned the hangar, but he didn't see a ship. He assumed it was just invisible, cloaked under its active camouflage. His eyes squinted to find the outline of a Chameleon, but he only saw a set of double doors leading out from the airy space.

"So what have you got for us? Recon? Going behind enemy lines?" It being Friday night, Neil figured he had the weekend to save some sort of botched mission before the end of Janey's karate tournament. "It would rule if we could make it back by Sunday at sevenish. It's pizza night."

Neil and his friends already proved video gamers could handle anything, so he assumed their second mission should be a piece of cake.

"But more important, I can't wait to get back in a

Chameleon," Neil said, miming the controls of a phantom jet, "and to fly with you again, obviously."

"Well, about that . . . ," Jones replied, the two walking in stride under the fluorescent glow of the hangar's interior. They were nearly to the building's center as the huge exterior door finally clanked shut. "How'd you fare on that game I sent you?"

"Oh, Shuttle Fury?" Neil said, remembering his copy of the game, and the juice box that was still on top of it. "Um, well, you know, pretty good. I didn't get a chance to totally 'finish it,' so to speak, but—"

"I know what you mean," Jones interrupted. "Figured I'd send it to you all on the off chance anybody could beat the blasted thing."

"Nobody ever has?" Neil asked, anxious to move the subject of conversation away from his Shuttle Fury score, or lack thereof. "I mean . . . right! No way anybody has beaten that thing."

"It's impossible. Now just more of a hazing ritual. Something the Force gives to all new test pilots on their first day," Jones said, his voice echoing off the ceiling's rippled sheet metal.

"So you've played it?" Neil asked.

"Some. Not well, though. When I play it's more like Shuttle Furious," Jones answered, producing a chuckle from Neil. They'd reached the center of the hangar, and busy technicians buzzed around them as Jones stood still. "But I figured I'd send it. Call it a hunch."

Neil's forehead crinkled.

"A hunch?" Neil asked, unsure what he meant.

Jones pointed up. Above Neil hung a banner with a blue circle and futuristic lettering.

"Welcome to NASA, Neil Andertol," Jones said. "Or should I say: potential Astronaut Andertol."

Neil's eyebrows arched up.

Astronaut Andertol.

The title sounded surreal, especially for someone who had been called Boogercheeks earlier in the day.

"Now let's get moving; we've got work to do."

Neil felt his stomach drop, and he was still a long way from outer space.

CHAPTER 4

NEIL GATHERED HIS THOUGHTS, OR AT LEAST SOME OF THEM, and followed Jones through a twisting hallway. It branched out from the huge open space of the hangar, and Jones cut through it in quick strides. Neil was reminded of the mysterious military base he had woken up in months ago. The walls and floor were so similar, Neil almost wondered if it was the same place—or the same interior designer, at least.

Jones abruptly turned another corner, and the hallway came to a dead end. He pushed open a heavy door, revealing a long glossy table full of friendly faces.

"Jones! ManofNeil!" shouted an energetic Robert Hurbigg, or just Biggs for short. Biggs made a hand signal that looked like a dying finger puppet.

"Biggs! Everybody else!" Neil said, a goofy smile stuck on his face. He looked down the two rows of seats, both dramatically lit by the ceiling's track lighting. Neil was surprised, but happy, to see that all his friends had arrived before him. He was realizing just how much he'd missed everyone.

"Glad you could join us," said a distinguished-looking African American man in a deep-blue suit. He stood behind a podium at the opposite end of the long table.

"Glad I could, too," Neil said. "You guys didn't get started without me, did you?"

The man said nothing but gestured to the empty seat at the end of the table closest to the door.

Okay, maybe not the best time for jokes.

Neil took the seat next to Yuri, who was clad in gray sweatpants with a velvety cape. The pale dungeon master gave a nod of his greasy forehead, and Neil scanned the ten other faces lining the table.

They were the same video gamers who'd been previously recruited by the military for Neil's last mission.

They'd all been deemed the best, based on their top scores from a leaked military flight simulator, Chameleon. The scores were apparently good enough to merit a second chance at saving the world.

Across from Neil sat the identical faces of brothers Dale and Waffles, the tips of their round ears peeling with sunburn. Incognito superhero Jason 2 smiled at Neil, a glittery black costume peeking out from under his shirt collar.

Next to him Jason 1, sporting a freshly cut fade, threw a make-believe football at Neil. It may have actually been a make-believe cantaloupe, but Neil mimicked catching whatever it was with both hands.

"Greetings, Lord Neil!" whispered Riley, a doughy boy wearing a dirty yellow tunic. As he bowed with a royal flourish, Neil wondered who was left at his Renaissance fair to act as swineherd.

"Greetings, my fair pig wrangler," Neil responded. Jones and the well-dressed stranger were busy talking, so Neil's eyes darted to tally the remaining crew. There was JP waving hello in a sweet Taiwanese soccer jersey, and Corinne in the next swiveling chair. Her hair was wrapped into two spongy buns, and she wore a new pair of dark-brown plastic glasses. She mouthed, "Hi, Neil!" He was a bit disappointed when she didn't spell anything using her body, the source of her spelling bee YouTube fame.

Neil locked eyes with Trevor, who offered a kind of long, extended blink. Neil knew not to expect much more from someone he classified as a certifiable wiener.

From the far end of the table, Neil felt another pair of eyes on him. He turned to see Sam staring straight at him. Her shiny brown hair was now tucked up in a pony-tail, the front chopped into a curled row of bangs. She smiled weirdly, doing her best to hide two rows of new braces. They were silver, with tiny sparks of orange stuck to the front of each tooth.

While Neil was happy to see everyone, it was Sam who made him feel a slight buzzing in his fingertips. As his palms grew sweaty, for reasons Neil wasn't altogether sure of, Jones's voice broke his trance.

"Will do, sir," said Jones. He stepped back from the podium, nodded at the man in the blue suit, and headed for the room's exit.

"Wait, you're leaving?" blurted Biggs, his face dis-tressed. "But who can I steal sunflower seeds from?"

"Keep it together, Hurbigg; you'll be fine. Keep an eye out for this one, Draymond," said Jones, playfully pointing toward Biggs. As he stood in the doorway, he gave a salute. "You're in good hands, team."

And with a swish of the doors, their former leader was gone.

Well. This doesn't seem to be going like I'd expected.

Neil and the others directed their eyes back to the man in the suit.

"The name's Commander Draymond Finch," the man said after clearing his throat. "And NASA needs you all."

The group remained hushed. *Why would NASA need video gamers?*

Even though he'd barely spoken, Neil thought Finch seemed friendly. His voice was much calmer than Jones's, plus he didn't have that pulsing jaw muscle thing happening.

Finch had short hair shaped like a fuzzy horseshoe that left the top of his head bald and shiny. His bushy mustache and eyebrows were speckled with gray streaks. Neil wondered if he used some kind of bowling alley grease to give his scalp such a radiant glow.

"Normally I'd offer a proper introduction, but there's no time to waste."

Neil had been waiting for months for someone to deny information because time was of the essence.

"You all should know that Jones and I flew on our first five tours as soldiers, served together as test pilots, and I trust him like a brother," said Finch. "So when we discussed our situation, he convinced me you all could be our only chance of success. Because honestly, we're out of options."

No pressure or anything.

The overhead lights dimmed, and above the podium a crystal clear 3-D projection appeared. It was a sleek blue orb visible from all directions, and it depicted a rotating ship, which resembled a futuristic Chameleon fused with a standard space shuttle.

Uh-oh. That looks a lot like Shuttle Fury.

Finch clicked a button on the tiny remote he clutched in his left hand and rolled video footage of a rocket preparing for launch. The time stamp on the clip was from the same day, just earlier in the morning.

"As you can see, today we were set to launch one of our top-of-the-line spaceplanes, a model called the

Whiptail. The craft handles similarly to the Chameleons you've piloted, but it can withstand the rigors of space.

"This particular ship is the *Newt*. It can reach Mach 25 in less than a minute and even function like an airplane in Earth's atmosphere," Finch explained as the video playing showed preflight preparation accompanied by the audio of crew-member radio transmissions.

"In other words, it's expensive," said Trevor.

"You could say that," Finch replied. "But just after oh-nine-hundred, an hour before the scheduled launch, the not-cheap spacecraft became compromised, along with our entire computer system. The only video we could recover is from an outdoor security camera."

"You mean, like, you were hacked?" asked JP, his huge brain already working overtime.

"We believe, yes. Whoever it was took total control of our operating systems, completely untraced."

Neil watched the idling rocket, fixated as confusion and mayhem broke out over the radio frequency. The rocket attached to the shuttle began to fire, and it quickly lifted toward the stratosphere.

"Who's flying this shuttle? Who approved this launch!?" came a distressed voice from the recording. As voices were replaced by the explosive sounds of chemical rocket propulsion, Neil watched the graceful liftoff, following the white plumes of smoke that streaked from the ground far into the air. It looked like a shooting star.

Wait a second—that's what I saw at the planetarium!

Neil hadn't witnessed a rare asteroid or shooting star but an even rarer space shuttle hijack.

"You mean, this was just stolen, like my sister's bike outside of a pool hall?" chimed Biggs.

"And didn't the shuttle program end?" questioned Sam, who was pretty much an encyclopedia of knowledge on space, fossils, and old military slang for taking a dump.

"Yes, technically," Finch said to Sam before turning to Biggs. "And I'm not here to provide excuses: the ship was stolen, plain and simple. The first reported incident of grand space theft. Involving our most technologically advanced craft to date."

Neil could tell Finch was a bit embarrassed to admit his mission was a failure, and having to tell Jones probably didn't help. Messing up was never fun in front of friends, especially ones who can spit sunflower shells at you.

"But . . . ," Finch said, "we're proposing a mission, the likes of which has never been attempted before—using an old experimental prototype of our stolen spacecraft. The *Fossil*. While it isn't exactly a conventional ship, it should still be able to get you to space and back and retrieve our stolen ship."

Not conventional? Is that an adult term for death trap?

"You mean, we're going to space?" Sam asked.

"Yes."

Space.

But Neil felt strangely confident. If he could fly a Chameleon through the clouds with ease, doing so without the constant nuisance of gravity should be easy. Right?

CHAPTER 5

"SO WE'D BE ASTRONAUTS?" NEIL ASKED IN DISBELIEF.

"That depends. By now, I assume all you recruits are experts at Shuttle Fury," Commander Finch said.

Neil felt sweat prick out of every pore on his body, his stomach twisting like a wet towel. He was the opposite of an expert at Shuttle Fury. He was an expert at being the worst.

"I know I'm taking Jonesey's word on a lot of this, but we at least need one hundred and fifty hours logged from you all on Shuttle Fury. You've all at least managed that, correct?"

Finch's eyes scanned the group and abruptly turned to Neil.

"Of course," Neil squeaked out the lie. "Sir."

Give or take 149 hours. . . . It's not too late to back out, right? Everyone would understand.

"Commander Finch, sir," Neil said, clearing his throat with a nervous cough. "Why us? Why can't you guys just use normal astronauts?"

Neil's friends shot him a look, like he'd just asked the worst question in existence. Obviously everyone wanted to go to space.

Finch twitched his nose and mustache like some kind of furry animal. "It's all part of Plan 'Zee," Finch reassured, which wasn't all that assuring. The group paused as it felt like a dark cloud passed over their ideas of glory.

"We're down to Plan Z? What happened to A through Y?" asked Jason 2.

"Great. You're already thinking like astronauts, recruits," Finch said. "You must question everything."

"Well, we're questioning, my man!" said Waffles. "Because I could make Plan W happen if need be."

Finch gestured for both Waffles and the incognito

superhero to calm down. Neil wasn't sure what Plan W would look like exactly, but it probably involved gallons of face paint Waffles likely smuggled with him.

"Plan 'Zee. Short for 'chimpanzee,'" Finch explained, clicking the remote still cradled in his hand. Another, tinier craft appeared in the blue-projected orb. "Recruits, let me introduce you to the *Fossil*. The only Whiptail shuttle we have left. An experimental model, as I told you. It's a smaller, simpler design."

"The *Fossil* was the first Whiptail to be manufactured, made to cut rapidly through deep space," Finch said. "It's designed to be flown by a squad of highly trained chimpanzees."

"Is that what you guys think of us? A bunch of dirty apes?" shouted Waffles.

"Easy, Charlie. Because it was designed for primates, the ship's height clearance is far too short for any astronaut," said Finch. "You're the only people with any sort of applicable flight hours logged who are capable of flying it."

"Oh. Cool," said Waffles.

Neil knew piloting a vehicle meant for apes was a new twist, but the mission was suddenly too tempting to back out now—if a chimp could fly the Whiptail, Neil could, too.

"We made the controls easy enough for chimpanzees to understand. From what Jones has told me, you all are an impressive lot. I have full faith in you," Finch explained.

Neil knew the blessing from a NASA commander was a big deal, and he was pretty sure it was all going to be fine. No one would just send kids into space unless it was completely safe. Right?

"But to be clear, the *Fossil* is our only chance at stopping the thieves who have our ship," Finch said. "There's no telling what they intend to do with it, but we basically have a craft with enough explosive liquid fuel to act as its own nuclear device. Big enough to destroy an entire country."

Gotcha. Okay, so maybe not completely *safe.*

"Commander Finch? How are we supposed to find a missing rocket that could be anywhere in *space*?" Trevor demanded, probably using arguing tactics picked up from his lawyer father.

"Yeah!" Corinne added. "I can't even find my mom in a grocery store. How are we going to find anybody in space? It's huge!"

"Once you're in orbit, your rocket will initiate a specifically tuned radar to lead you directly to the missing spacecraft," Finch responded. "While the thieves hacked almost everything else, from space we can still ping the missing ship's homing beacon to force its coordinates and catch up to it in the *Fossil*. It's the only ship we have that can keep up with the *Newt*'s speed."

Across the table, Sam raised her hand with a question.

"Yes . . . ," Finch said, skimming his manifest of young soldiers. "Samantha?"

"Pretty much everybody calls me Sam, but whichever you prefer, sir," she replied. "More important, how are we actually going to go to space within twenty-four hours? Astronauts train for years before they attempt something even remotely close to this."

Neil watched the NASA commander subtly shift. He knew Sam had a great point and that her knowledge of space far surpassed his own. Up until the age of seven, for example, he had sincerely believed the moon was made of cheese, or some kind of lactose-free space equivalent.

"Good question," Finch responded, lowering his clicker-wielding hand onto the podium to give Sam his full attention. "We have data that insists this experience shouldn't be harder on you all than your previous mission. And I'll be right with you to ensure you're all okay," Finch said. "But I can't stress enough the importance of this mission's success. You are the only people alive able to return our stolen ship."

Neil knew after a speech like that, there was no turning back.

"Now, as Sam so astutely put it, you'll be in training for the next twenty-four hours. We'll meet up with my mission capsule communicator, or CAPCOM, Colonel Dallas Bowdin. If any of you cannot pass training, we won't send you on the mission, simple as that. It would be a risk to the crew and mission. These are standard rules for all astronauts."

Astronaut. Neil repeated the word over and over in his head, his heartbeat steadily racing in excitement. Space was the ultimate adventure, the only place left for true exploration. He knew he had to prove himself worthy of the title.

But there was a level of danger to the mission that Finch hadn't expanded upon yet.

Who actually steals a space shuttle in the first place?

"Tomorrow, all of you who passed training will

board the *Fossil* to pursue and recover our stolen ship, the *Newt*," Finch said, discontinuing the video projection. He turned to the group, his words stern. "There is no dishonor if you want to leave now."

Everyone silently listened for movement—but not a noise was made.

Silent, just like in space. Where we're going. In real life.

"Well then, it's settled, recruits," said Finch. "Welcome to NASA. We've got some work to do."

CHAPTER

6

★ ★ ★

NEIL LOOKED AT HIS NEW NASA-ISSUED WATCH. HE LOOS-
ened it a notch and watched the face blink to read 20:53.
He wanted to be early for the start of training, something
he thought Commander Finch would appreciate. He also
hoped timeliness would be valued more than mastery of
the video game simulator he should have been playing
all summer.

Before darting out of the conference room, Finch
had handed everyone a short test to complete. It was
full of random questions about space, medical attention,

and physics. Neil took his time, knowing science wasn't exactly his strongest subject. Only last year he had asked for dismissal from biology to take gym for two periods, which was saying something.

So while everyone else finished and headed to the locker room, Neil was last. He did a quick change into his powder-blue uniform in a bathroom stall. Within a minute Neil was squeaking down the facility in double-knotted black boots. He stood by the double doors leading into the hangar, where Finch had instructed everyone to meet. Busy technicians ran past him in pairs but saluted the lone gamer as they passed.

"Mr. Andertol," said a woman a few inches taller than Neil, clad in a sterilized white jumpsuit, as if she were touring a chocolate factory.

"Miss, ah, Space-traveling Astronaut," Neil replied with a salute, wishing her uniform had some sort of name patch. She smiled and kept moving down the hallway, her hair neatly tucked into a bleached white hairnet.

Neil's eyes drifted from the hustling NASA employees to the walls around him. They were lined with a slew of mission achievements and memorials; each corridor was dedicated to another feat of science and space. This was even better than the Greater Colorado Museum and Planetarium and Homestyle Buffet. It was like an astronaut hall of fame.

Closest to Neil were photos of NASA's astronaut classes, framed and hung in order by year. Ranging from 1959 to the present, each photo showed a smiling group of jumpsuit-wearing astronauts, all in a hangar, space station, or science lab. Only recent shots showcased astronauts in their full suits and helmets, and they all featured cheesy smiles, posing in front of the blue NASA logo. It was reassuring to see that brave and fearless galaxy adventurers still looked awkward on class photo day.

I should see what Commander Finch looked like with *hair.*

Scanning each photograph intently, Neil tried to find the broad shoulders and impressively square jaw of his new commanding officer. His search soon stopped at 2001 and the glistening, curly locks of a young Draymond Finch.

He stood alongside three other astronauts. One was a strapping man with a neck like a small birch tree, and another a bookish astronaut who was about a foot shorter. The only lady of the class had curly blond hair and a beautiful, slightly rectangular face.

"Can't believe it's been so long," Finch said, sidling up to Neil.

"Since that hairstyle was okay? I know," Neil said, getting Finch to crack a half smile for the first time.

"Well, that, too," Finch replied, the two of them standing in pools of reflected light on the shiny floor. "Our class was the best NASA had, or has, ever seen."

"Who were the others?" Neil asked. "And were you the best? I bet you were the best."

Finch exhaled, but the half smile was gone, almost turning into a half frown.

"No, that honor belonged to Astronaut Jon Dewett," Finch said, gesturing to the man on his right in the picture. "Best pilot and astronaut I've ever seen."

He was the taller, olive-skinned man from Finch's graduating class. He was equally mustachioed, with brown hair that tapered back into a tasteful mullet. From what Neil had seen, 2001 was a pretty rough year in terms of hairstyles.

"I'm the only one still with NASA."

"Really? Where is he now?"

"Something of a disagreement. The participants of the program parted ways, and he left for the private space race." Finch groaned. "Commercial missions, the wave of the future."

"And who were the others? Did they go with him?"

"Clint and Elle Minor. They were married during training," Finch said, his normally stoic voice cracking slightly. "They piloted the first manned mission to Mars."

He turned to the wall opposite him and Neil. It displayed a framed photograph of the married astronauts, both climbing into a craft that looked like the stolen Whiptail from the video Finch played earlier. It wasn't as streamlined, but it was still similar to the craft now joyriding through the galaxy.

"Lost in space—terribly tragic. Almost a year ago to the week," Finch said delicately. "They were in the first human-sized Whiptail we constructed, *The Golden Gecko*. With our new technology, one-way missions were thought to be a thing of the past. They left behind two kids."

"Did you know them? The kids?" Neil asked.

"I only met them a handful of times," Finch answered before erupting into a small coughing fit. "Excuse me for a moment. Think I need a little water. Back at twenty-one hundred hours—you know, I've heard a lot of good things about you, Andertol."

None of them regarding shuttle simulators, I hope!

The commander exited the hallway, and Neil was alone once again. He stared at the faces of immortalized space travelers and wondered if any of them had also lied during the application process.

Oh, the Minors.

The name of the missing couple struck a bell. Neil remembered his parents glued to the nonstop footage of the first manned mission to Mars, and when it went awry. Neil's mom watched all day, hoping a distress call or radio signal would offer their whereabouts.

Unfortunately Neil had a pretty good score going in Chameleon, so his attention was elsewhere. After a few weeks, his mother finally gave up hope, along with everybody else.

"Neil Andertol, you slippery serpent!" Biggs yelled, appearing from the locker room to wrap Neil in a bear hug.

Biggs looked at least two inches taller, like a stretched-out version of himself with a pointier Adam's apple. He'd apparently hit something of a growth spurt over the summer, but still looked like a shaggy, unwashed mop that had come to life.

"Biggs! So good to see you, too," Neil said, muffled by his friend's chest. He pulled his head back and took a gasp of fresh air. "Just don't crush my lungs with your giant adult man arms. Did you get that operation where they put horse bones in your body to make you taller?"

Biggs dropped Neil and straightened his jumpsuit.

"No, but good to know that's always an option for later in life," Biggs said to Neil. "Man, Neil Andertol. In the flesh. There's so much I want to catch up on with you. You gotta see the new game—Harris and I are really close to having something!"

"Oh, that's right! You're actually helping with *Feather Duster 2*?" Neil questioned, remembering Biggs's offer of support to Harris for all smell-related game additions.

"It's been a blast. Harris is, like, really smart. I'm talking Wikipedia smart," said Biggs. He probably had Jones pull a few strings to get him off the hook for capturing a Chameleon. He wasn't a truly evil person, really.

"Your smell thing is working? You ever get past bacon?" asked Neil, remembering Biggs's last enterprise.

"Smells . . . well, smells are getting there—maybe a bit too much wet-dog smell at times, but we're close."

"Dude, that's so awesome. I can't wait to play it. And

smell the parts that don't smell like golden retrievers."

"And that's not even the good news!" Biggs said, his face lighting up. "You, sir, are looking at a man making a new language."

"Like a whole new one?" Neil wondered, waving quick hellos to the rest of the group as they trickled into the hallway. Everyone tried doing a slow-motion, space movie walk, decked out in official-looking uniforms.

"Are you making up new words?"

"We'll use standard words, all the greatest hits. It's a new sign language," Biggs said, moving his hands like two swimming octopi.

"Right now people in America only have one option for sign language. So I'm making The Universal Biggs Language, or TUBL for short. For anyone interested in switching things up. Or learning thirteen different hand symbols for the word *pancake*."

"It sounds to be a noble enterprise, Master Biggs," said Riley, his pudgy frame stuffed into a half-zipped jumpsuit.

"Riley!" Neil exclaimed.

"Salutations, my fellow space cadets!" Riley shouted, tugging on a sleeve to get his outfit to cooperate. Trevor, the Jasons, and Yuri joined everyone, forming two make-shift lines at opposite sides of the hallway.

"Been a bit tough with long-sleeved garments since the stocks," said Riley, in his comforting but bizarre way of speaking.

"Like, the stock market?" Trevor questioned Riley.

"No, 'twas out in the town square's stocks for a few moons," Riley replied, referring to a wooden contraption, designed for public ridicule, that locked his head and hands in place. "Standard Renaissance fair punishment for an undutiful swineherd. I'll be fine, just have a fanciful popping sound in one shoulder is all."

Formerly Neil's online nemesis, Trevor was more filled out since the beginning of summer, having lost a bit of the baby fat from his face. His freckled cheeks were subtly tan, and he still had what most people would consider a huge head.

"I had a hunch they'd want us to beat that Shuttle Fury game," Trevor said to Neil, closing in on Neil's spot at the front of the line. "You didn't finish it either, did you?"

"No, not really. More like Shuttle Furious, am I right?" Neil answered, completely ripping off Jones's joke. The group laughed, and Neil felt a bit of unearned relief. The truth was getting easier to twist with each pass.

"I figured you couldn't beat that space thing. Nobody could; it's impossible," Trevor said. "I tried to find any kind of cheat code just to see what happens in the end but couldn't find anything online. Nobody's beaten it— that game must be completely top secret. Or just so awful nobody played it."

Neil nodded slowly, choosing not to reveal the true origin of the game. It felt cheap to steal Jones's joke one second and credit him the next.

Sam and Corinne filtered in from the girls' locker room, gleefully catching up with each other. Neil wanted to go run and talk to Sam and poke fun at her braces, but farther down the hall appeared a determined Finch. Sam stopped in her tracks at the sound of the commander's voice.

"This way, everyone," said Finch, and strode toward a red emergency exit. It was the opposite direction from the hangar, where Neil had thought a sweet aircraft would be waiting for them.

Must be a ship already warmed up outside.

The group hustled down the hall, each one doing

their best not to joyously dash toward whatever adventure awaited.

"You guys talkin' about the NASA game?" whispered Yuri, strands of greasy, long black hair covering just his right eye. "I couldn't make it much past halfway. Too hard."

"It might be the hardest game I've ever played," said JP, whose gelled hair still retained the properties of cave stalagmites.

Jason 1, now wearing a handmade beanie, and Jason 2, probably wearing a superhero costume under his jumpsuit, groaned in unison.

"Yeah, I got to that warp speed level, but everything was super difficult and technical," Jason 2 chimed in, his boots looking to be triple-knotted.

Finch pushed through the emergency door and onto a large patch of grass softly lit by a half-moon.

The group hesitantly followed as Finch continued off paved ground into lush Bermuda grass. With a few more strides he was almost to the edge of the salty ocean waves, which Neil had smelled earlier.

"Excuse me, sir? Aren't we supposed to be training to fly space shuttles or something?" asked Corinne. "I think they're that way—in the hangar. Where shuttles live."

Neil agreed, and also wondered which ocean it was. The tops of waves curled over in plateaus of white water as moonlight melted onto everything. If Neil were home like any other Friday night, he'd be hours into a game of Chameleon.

A bubbling and gurgling started about thirty yards from shore. It charted a course toward Neil, slowly revealing the top of a grayish-black vehicle.

It was a stealthy craft that shared sleek angles with the design of the Chameleon and Whiptail, but was shaped a bit like a stingray. Maybe twenty yards across, its thin edges tapered up to a bulging center. What would normally be the head of the sea animal was the cabin of the ship, its eyes the cockpit's two windows.

"NASA public transportation," Finch said. "Always on time."

The craft smoothly spun in the water, and the main cabin's rear hatch opened toward Finch and his gaming crew. Saltwater beaded off its shiny exterior as Finch stepped onto the back of the ship.

It was completely empty, apparently controlled by

autopilot. Flashing computers lined the walls, and two silver poles ran the length of the ceiling. Neil figured they were for balance while standing, as he didn't see any seats. All twelve recruits followed their commander, who sealed the door shut once Riley finished climbing aboard.

"Recruits, this is the *Ray*. Our lift to the SQUID," Finch said.

"You guys *really* have a thing with the animal names, don't you?" Neil said as Finch gave him a glare. "You *did* say to keep questioning."

"What kind of miles per gallon you get on this beast?" interrupted Waffles, his hyperactive body pressed up against the unstaffed control panel at the front of the vessel. With thirteen passengers, space was limited.

"Submarines don't go by miles, dude," Dale said to his brother. "Maybe nautical miles?"

"And did you say 'squid'? I'm vegetarian. Just so you know," said Sam.

"And I haven't been eating anything with more than three vowels in it, so just something else to keep in mind," Biggs added. "Oh, I'll make that a question. Do you have any space oats on your SQUID?"

"Okay, we're getting the hang of questioning every-thing. We can save some for later," said Finch with a hint of exasperation in his voice. "And lucky for you we've got freeze-dried PB&J on the SQUID, which stands for Space-Quality Underwater Immersion Domicile.

"Most astronauts train there for a week or so before their mission. Our training facility offers the most realis-tic space training in a zero-g, underwater environment. Astronauts used to do immersion training in huge pools, and that was merely scratching the surface. One night here, and we'll see who among you is cut out to be an astronaut."

Now we're talking.

CHAPTER 7

AS THE SHIP'S HATCH CLOSED WITH A SOFT HISS, ENGINES below the floor buzzed to life, and Neil could feel vibrations through his thick boots. The craft lurched from the shoreline and plunged back underwater. Floodlights on the front of the ship sent schools of tiny shimmering fish darting in opposite directions.

Neil watched the submersible cruise toward an underwater structure awash in fuzzy lighting. It had a giant circular main level and four tunnel arms that extended down into separate smaller structures. It really looked like a squid with tentacles.

"This is awesome," muttered JP.

"This already feels like space," said Jason 1. Neil agreed.

The vehicle drew closer and entered an air lock underneath the main structure. The entrance resealed, and the water in the transition room flooded out.

The room was sparse, with just a sturdy yellow-and-black door marking the way out.

"And we're home," said Finch. "After me, recruits. No time to waste." The hydraulic door of the shuttle opened, and the group rushed out into the small windowless air lock. Finch placed his thumb against a scanner, and the door slid open after a series of beeps.

Neil wondered what might happen to unauthorized thumbprints.

"Some extensive underwater security, Commander Finch," JP remarked.

"Well, a lot of unsavory people would be very interested in the information and training that happens down here. Some things are best left classified," the NASA official responded.

Finch moved across the threshold of the doorway into the SQUID, interior lighting illuminating the shiny silver-and-blue floors and walls. The place was pristine and very new, with the main section of the SQUID serving as a kitchen, library, and classroom. The main floor had the NASA logo emblazoned in sparkly paint, and another blue-suited NASA official was standing in wait.

She had short black hair, which was lightly hair-sprayed and parted to one side. Her skin was a radiant light brown, and she had eyebrows that looked like sharp apostrophes.

"Good to see you, Dallas," said Finch.

"Sir," saluted the soldier opposite the commander. More NASA specialists and scientists scurried around her in all directions, flying past like worker bees. They wore the same sterilized white outfits from before, carrying laptops and messy spools of diagnostic cables.

"Any leads on our hackers?" Finch asked.

"None yet, but we're working nonstop, sir."

"Recruits, allow me to introduce you to Dallas Bowdin, my right-hand woman and chief CAPCOM, or capsule communicator," said Finch to his group of twelve. "She runs operations on the SQUID."

She looked to have the same stern eyes and gritty disposition as Jones.

And there's that clenched jaw muscle!

"Welcome to the SQUID, ladies and gentlemen," she said, her voice slightly raspy, like Sam's. "Now down to business."

Neil's eyes darted quickly around the room, watching the contained insanity held within the underwater facility. There were no more than ten NASA workers motoring around the SQUID, but they moved like crazed speed walkers.

He counted six separate doorways out of the main structure. Two were marked as the men's and women's barracks, with the others most likely leading to the tentacles.

"As you'll see, each tunnel leads down to a unique training simulation," Bowdin explained. "We'll start tonight, and you should all have enough time to complete each section by tomorrow morning. Ideally, we'll be able to determine crew positions by training scores. But first things first: in twenty minutes, you've all got a date with the Vomit Comet."

Neil looked at his watch, and he couldn't help but feel a little uneasy and reluctant. Not only would this be his first date, but he didn't necessarily trust methods of transportation that spoke so freely of puking.

"For now, everybody find bunks. And I need two volunteers," Finch said to the group, pointing at Sam and Neil. "Our first duo on kitchen duty. Just grab some snacks from the kitchen for after the Vomit Comet. You're going to love our freeze-dried cuisine. We make sure to fine-tune every recipe. I did a four-hour debrief on the chicken Alfredo alone."

"As long as it's better than those MREs, we'll love it," said Waffles.

"Ugh. It's been years since my Air Force days, and I still have nightmares about those. You kids are in for a treat."

Finch began rounds to tour the facility, checking illuminated touch pads built into the walls of the SQUID. Biggs and JP headed for the bunks, while Dale and the rest followed Finch, eager to see the rest of the secret underwater station.

"So is one of these things where we train to fight sharks? Or did I hear you incorrectly," trailed Waffles's voice as the group plodded into a corridor.

Soon Neil and Sam were left alone in the main circular room.

They wandered toward the kitchen, mesmerized by

their surreal enclosure. Glass skylights overhead let the natural moonlight mix with the blue LED bulbs lining the room, and the two friends roamed the SQUID in silence, reflections of water dancing on the floor below.

While Sam was, by all accounts, Neil's best friend, there was an awkward silence hanging between them. It wasn't like they hadn't spoken for a while, as Neil received Sam's message earlier in the day; it just felt like forever since they had actually *talked*. Just about games, or their day, or being grounded for triple-knotting a younger sister's karate belt.

Neil remembered entire weekends spent talking with Sam, and now he was struggling to come up with a sentence.

He turned to Sam and finally opened his mouth. He mustered a sputtering wheeze.

"You okay there, champ?" Sam laughed.

"I was just gonna say you look pretty official," Neil said to his friend in her new NASA duds. "Like you were meant to wear that jumpsuit."

Sam's hair seemed to be longer and shinier than before, like one of the actresses in a shampoo commercial who constantly twirled her hair while holding a tiny dog.

"Astronaut Neil Andertol has a pretty good ring to it, too," said Sam. "Seems much cooler than just a plain old pilot."

"Hey, don't hate on pilots," Neil replied. "But Astronaut Gonzales sounds pretty good, too. You play that bad boy in Scrabble, and there's some points comin' your way."

What? Was that a Scrabble joke?

"Neil, you are the weirdest person I know. In a good way," she said, her soft brown eyes sparkling. "And I really think I'm ready for space. I've been practicing all summer on that simulator."

"Oh, that's where you've been when you were abandoning me to fly with only Biggs?"

"Oh, whatever," she replied. "You're like the king of that game. I'm sure noobs were lining up to copilot."

Neil could only wish she was right. He'd spent an entire summer buckling down to master Chameleon, and it seemed like the only people who talked to him were his babysitter, mom, and the beef jerky–loving Tyler.

"And my Chameleon skills got a little rusty over the summer. Shuttle Fury controls took some getting used to."

"Oh, right," Neil said, unaware the controls were any

different. He leaned in toward Sam. "Jones actually told me it's impossible. Just something they give people as a joke."

Sam looked taken aback, her eyes flaring a bit.

"Really?"

"Totally. I don't even think we need to worry about that game," Neil reassured. "They obviously wanted us because of our Chameleon skills."

"Hm, yeah maybe, I guess."

"Anyways, I heard about a weird space thing today. Made me think of you."

"Ha, you mean like a NASA commander giving us a whole speech about a shuttle being stolen?"

"Ugh, that's not what I mean, a *different* space thing," Neil playfully shot back. "A crater. I can't remember that name, though. Like, 'Chicken Laboos.' Is the Chicken Laboos crater a thing?"

"Pretty sure that's a fast-food value meal." Sam laughed. "But I think I get what you're saying. That asteroid that hit in Mexico, right?"

"Yeah! Man, you really do know all things space."

"Some. There's quite a lot of it to know," she replied.

"I bet the Question Commander knows most

everything, though," Neil said, referring to their new quirky superior.

"Everything? They don't even know who took their spaceship."

Well, good point.

"I mean, yeah," Neil said. "But Jones had no clue a mad genius video gamer was the reason for our last mission either, right?"

Sam seemed hesitant to agree.

"First, let's not get carried away calling that Harris kid a genius," she joked. "And I'll admit there's a chance you could be right. Just getting a weird gut feeling, I guess."

"You know what's best for weird gut feelings? Freeze-dried ice cream," said Neil as he pulled open a drawer in the futuristic kitchen area. Inside were silver-packaged bricks of rocky road and Neapolitan stacked in neat rows.

"Think we should wait until after a training simulator named for puke?" Sam debated.

"A little bit won't hurt."

Neil tore two open, and the friends took bites into the soft fake ice cream. Crumbles of dehydrated dessert fell onto their uniforms.

"Thanks, Neil," Sam said, pulling out enough packages for everyone else.

Neil smiled and nervously brushed off his suit.

Moonlight glimmered through waves and small schools of fish, and Neil's thoughts went up above the surface. He gazed upward through a glass bubble above the kitchen, which magnified the ocean above.

"Apart from skilled, professionally trained astrophysicists and astronauts, there's nobody else I'd rather venture into space with than Neil Andertol: ice cream taste tester of the future."

"That's Astronaut Neil Andertol."

Sam groaned, her mouth half-full of powdered ice cream.

"One thing at a time, hero. One thing at a time."

CHAPTER

8

"RECRUITS. IT'S TIME TO SEE HOW YOU HANDLE THE VOMIT Comet," said Finch to his twelve potential spacewalkers. They were in a staggered crescent, surrounding the NASA commander outside a training tentacle. It was a bulky white structure the size of a tank, with a sturdy metal door. "Any questions before we get started?"

While he wasn't going to ask, Neil was wondering if vomiting was simply encouraged, or a mandatory requirement.

"Yes, question?" said Finch to Biggs, who had raised his stringy arm in the air.

"Commander! Thanks. First-time caller, longtime listener," Biggs said. "I do have a pretty serious question for you in regard to this whole space mission."

"And that is?" said Finch, fidgeting. Neil wondered if Jones had given Finch some kind of advanced warning for life with Biggs. His questions were always . . . interesting.

"Well, sir, exactly how much urine will my space suit hold? Does that type of thing come standard in any and all jumpsuits, or will we have a separate session dealing with each uniform's urination logistics?" Biggs asked. "I've been reading a lot of online literature on the topic lately and could use some answers."

"I can reassure you all we'll thoroughly go over the specifics of the suit technology," replied Finch. He looked to see more hands raised with questions. Yuri and both Jasons' arms were stretched intently, hoping the tallest hand would have questions answered first.

"Everyone, if you have a question related to answering nature's call in zero gravity, please save it for later."

All raised hands slowly recoiled, except Sam's. She had a determined look on her face, and she coolly lowered her hand as Finch nodded to her.

"So is this a ship? Or just a place where new astronauts are made to toss their cookies?" Sam asked bluntly.

"A reduced-gravity simulation," Finch explained. "Designed to re-create a zero-g environment. The very kind you'll be encountering on your mission."

Neil liked how Finch seemed confident in everybody, that sending anyone home didn't appear to cross his mind.

"We used to simulate weightlessness out in the desert, flying up and down for hours," Finch said. "Now we have a deep-sea Vomit Comet, where there's no time limit on weightlessness."

How can I rent this thing for my birthday party?

It was like an amusement park ride, but better. Plus you didn't have to wait next to people with small tank tops and large amounts of body hair.

Neil couldn't wait to get inside, but he wondered if the amount of space ice cream he had eaten would pose a problem. Neil only had a package and a half, but he'd snuck Riley and Jason 2 a few, and they had gone hog wild.

"The clock is ticking, everyone," Finch said. "Now, after you, my recruits."

Sam was first to walk through the simulator's heavy door. Her hair swung back and forth with each step.

The interior was a giant white padded room with all sorts of handles and straps fastened to the walls and ceiling. It looked like a really wide school bus with no seats and a marshmallow interior.

"This will be a simulation of a sixty-parabola flight," Finch explained.

"Which means what exactly?" asked Waffles, tugging at a rope on a side of the room.

"It means this is gonna be awesome," said JP excitedly as his brain went through the calculations.

With a thud, the door to the simulation cabin shut, and the ground hummed with a hydraulic roar. Neil studied the walls and floor of the Vomit Comet closer, and saw every inch was speckled with tiny holes.

"When does the no-gravity part happen?" asked an impatient Yuri.

"Trust me. You'll know. Now hold on, people," said Finch. A high-pitched whirring began, and cool air rushed through the cabin. Neil felt like he was on a giant air hockey table.

Neil's body started to lift up from the floor.

"Whoa! This is unreal!" said Neil. It felt like he was rising out of his seat after hitting a huge hill on a roller coaster, only gravity wasn't pulling him back down.

Corinne was the first person to launch herself off the wall, floating through the cabin like a stuntwoman. Everyone followed her lead, and Neil felt like a superhero as he took a nosedive into a padded wall. He pushed off again, bending his knees to spring out. The whole experience was way more relaxing and comfortable than he'd expected.

"Easy, recruits," Finch urged.

Neil contorted his body, spinning midair like a figure skater. His stomach flitted a bit, but Neil felt like he could be weightless forever.

"And the simulation will end in ten . . . nine . . . eight . . . ," Finch said, counting down while looking at his watch. Neil did a quick back somersault and grabbed a strap near to the floor. Gravity took hold again, but Biggs, however, was still upside down.

"Ow," he grunted as his body crumpled to the floor.

"That's just round one," Finch said, assessing the condition of his astronaut candidates.

Most of Neil's friends were doing just fine, smiling

as if they were at an amusement park. Jason 2, however, was starting to look unwell. His eyes glassed over as he brought a hand to his stomach. Chocolate space ice cream clung to the corners of his mouth. Next to him, Yuri seemed worse.

"Another three minutes begins now," Finch said.

"Yuri, my dude, how you hanging in there?" Biggs asked, his hair branching out as gravity disappeared.

Yuri kept his lips pursed tight and made a motion to Biggs with both hands.

"Wait, you need something?" Biggs said, like a person deciphering a dog's barking. "What is it, boy? What's wrong? Trouble down at the old coal mine?"

"Here," said Sam, floating a barf bag to Yuri just before they were all witnesses to a lesson in applied zero-g physics.

"Oh, right," Biggs acknowledged. "Well, they don't call it a Vomit Comet for nothing. We've got our first member of the Spew Crew: Commander Yuri!"

"And possible second resident of the Yak Shack!" said Corinne as she watched Jason 2 reach for a barf bag. While he didn't puke, his body was turning all shades of green.

"Hey, Commander Vomit Comet? Update from the Spew Crew. I think we've got a Category Four, maybe Five with this one," said Biggs. He was looking at Yuri, whose body was a pale-yellow hue. In his stringy hands was a conspicuously lumpy waste receptacle.

Finch ended the simulation early, shutting off the high-powered vents on the simulator's control panel. Neil and the others slowly returned to the floor.

"Well, the good news is I think you're almost all cut out for our mission," Finch murmured, but nodded sadly at Yuri. "Unfortunately, we can't take him."

The crew was now down to eleven.

Finch opened the door and walked to the side of the Vomit Comet. He untied a stretcher and wheeled it to the doorway. There would be no extra lives or games to restart for Yuri, only a nightmarish lesson in human regurgitation.

CHAPTER

9

"OKAY, ANDERTOL," SAID FINCH. "THIS IS A PTT TO RUN through an EVA."

"Um, what?" replied Neil, standing alongside Biggs at the edge of a pool. Or at least what looked like a pool. It was a rectangle of open ocean water, all swishing around a submerged Whiptail. The bubble of the training tentacle must've been pressurized, or else the whole ocean would have been rushing inside.

"Sorry. We can get heavy on the abbreviations," Finch answered. "This is a part-task trainer, running a simulated extravehicular activity. Space walks. Or any-time you're outside of a craft in space. You should've seen something similar in Shuttle Fury."

"Oh. Yes, exactly," Neil fibbed. "More like Shuttle Furious, right?"

Biggs looked at Neil with a bit of joke déjà vu.

"That's a good one. I'll have to remember that." Finch chuckled. "But let's get moving. The rest of the group is with Dallas, running through other simulations. I'll be facilitating you all here in training tentacle three."

"Oh nice, that's always been my good-luck tentacle," Biggs said. The two gamers wore official space suits, complete with clear helmets that snapped into place. Finch communicated via a headset.

"I'm not sure what's about to happen, sir, but I just want to say I love it," said Biggs before cannonballing into the cool water.

Finch took a seat in a thin metal chair and planted both hands on a laptop computer. He began tapping keys as Neil splashed a toe through the water below.

"Hop on in, Andertol. The water's fine," said Biggs with a giddy excitement. Neil put his arms straight out to his sides and leaned forward with a belly flop.

"Now in this simulation, you'll both start at the starboard side of the ship," Finch said. Neil and Biggs swam over to the right side of the ship.

"The mission is to traverse the shuttle, close a leaking valve, and return to the airlock, sealing it without consequence. It's important to remain with your ship. Any second without contact could mean drifting out into space," Finch said over his headset. "You have eleven minutes of oxygen . . . starting now."

"Like, now or once we take a breath?" asked underwater Biggs.

"Ten fifty-five . . . ," replied Finch.

Neil turned to his shaggy-headed friend.

"Time to move, dude!"

The two began swinging around the waterlogged spaceship, making their way to its front. Neil propelled himself along the side of the ship, grabbing metal poles as if they were jungle vines.

This isn't so bad. Just keep your momentum going.

He guided himself to the nose of the ship and shinnied around the windows of the cockpit.

Just then, Finch's voice crackled over Neil's and Biggs's headsets.

"A patch of space junk has been detected in your orbit. You now have nine minutes to complete your mission," said Finch, relishing the drama of the simulation.

"Okay, let's motor," said Neil. Biggs agreed, and they pressed onward. Neil heard a broadcast in his ear.

"Specialist Andertol, you are the only one receiving this transmission. Your space suit is malfunctioning. Your helmet is slowly filling up with water from a clogged air filter."

Neil paused, wondering if he should return to the surface.

This is the whole challenge; you've got to keep going!

Biggs kept shuffling along the port side of the ship, and Neil slowly followed. He could see bubbles spraying out from the leaky valve they needed to reach.

"Specialist Andertol, your communication radio has been compromised by water damage."

So now I'm stuck out here without oxygen, and I can't talk?

Neil tugged hard at a metal pole bolted to the ship. He flew toward Biggs, snagging a corner of his oxygen pack.

"Specialist Andertol, your helmet is now half-filled with water. You've only got two minutes, maximum, of oxygen in reserve."

Neil turned to his friend and tried to communicate that his radio was broken. He kept pointing at his ears, making a slashing motion and an X with both forearms, but Biggs just didn't seem to get it.

Use The Universal Biggs Language!

What is The Universal Biggs Language?

Neil tried to imagine what would qualify as speech in his weird friend's head. He decided to make a gasping motion with his mouth, like a catfish. He flicked his tongue a lot, just to be dramatic.

"You okay, Neil?" said Biggs, gliding toward the problematic valve they were sent to fix.

Neil met eyes with Biggs, and his friend could instantly tell something was wrong.

"What's up, man? You okay?" Biggs asked.

Neil tried yelling, but Finch had disconnected his radio, just like what would happen in space. He knew he had to get himself out of the situation. There wasn't enough oxygen left for Neil to stay underwater while Biggs finished the mission, but he didn't know that. Neil had to let him know they needed to get back in the air lock immediately.

"Andertol, your suit is now rapidly filling up with

water from your cooling unit," Finch said over a speaker near Neil's head. "Your suit will be filled in less than forty-five seconds. What do you do?"

Neil threw caution to the wind and began trying to make hand movements that looked like horses or centaurs, or some other kind of mythical four-legged animal.

"Whoa! You in trouble, Neil?" Biggs yelled. He turned his attention from the bubbling valve outside of the fake Whiptail to his friend.

Neil made his mouth open wide, like a puffer fish suffocating onshore.

"You have a leak in your suit? Well, let's get back inside!" yelled Biggs, realizing the safety of his partner was more valuable than ship repairs. They floated back around the ship. Biggs ushered Neil into the ship's air lock, and Finch announced that the training was over.

Yellow-fin-wearing SCUBA divers, who had been overseeing the safety of the procedure, escorted Neil and Biggs to the water's surface.

"Well done, you two," the commander said. He typed a few more keystrokes into his laptop computer and stood up as Neil and Biggs were helped out from the pool.

"A huge key to being an astronaut is always thinking. Always being ready," Finch instructed, tapping a few buttons on his laptop. "And to—"

"Always ask questions," Neil and Biggs said in unison.

"We know," added Neil.

"Nicely done, Andertol," said Finch, preparing the simulation for the next pair of gamers. "Can't say I've ever seen an EVA quite like that, but the point is you passed. With flying colors, might I add."

Neil blushed. He felt ready. For what, he wasn't sure, but ready nonetheless.

"Dallas is still running simulations, so now's a good time for a nap. Go get some rest; we've got a planet to save."

"See you up in the main SQUID, Neil. I'm beat." Biggs walked off ahead, hoping to add the new gestures to The Universal Biggs Language before collapsing onto his bunk.

Neil nodded and confidently walked up to the central hub of the SQUID. But as he headed for the guys' bunks, he repeated what Finch just said.

What does he mean, "a planet to save"? Aren't we looking for a ship?

CHAPTER

10

"EVERYONE UP! THIS IS NOT A DRILL!" CAME AN EXPLOSIVE voice that echoed through every tentacle of the SQUID. It belonged to Dallas Bowdin, and it was interrupting some fantastic deep-sea shut-eye. Neil tried to wake up, but his eyes were stuck shut, refusing to open. Between eyelashes, he spied flashing blue emergency lights dotting the ceiling of the interior of the NASA complex. They pulsed on and off, twirling like tiny police sirens.

"What's going on?" asked a confused and groggy Biggs. "Aliens? Is it aliens?"

"Um, no. Not yet, at least." Neil sat up in bed and rubbed his eyelids with clenched fists. His eyes stung looking at his watch, which read 03:51.

"You guys want some questions? I've got a few," said a yawning Neil. "I'm beginning to question your guys' approach to a wake-up call. A fella needs time for a nice morning bag of dehydrated juice."

"Hurry up. It's our missing ship, the *Newt*," said Dallas from outside the room, heading to the center of the SQUID. Neil and Biggs scrambled to follow, with the others trailing behind. They had gotten into their bunks shortly after Neil and Biggs, and they wore the same exhausted expressions.

Dallas was waiting for the group with a few papers clutched in her hands. The fleet of NASA technicians bustled around her, heading to and from the *Ray*'s air lock. Sam and Corinne appeared from the girls' barracks, wearing matching baggy gray NASA T-shirts.

"So no continental breakfast?" asked a cranky Neil of Dallas. The kitchen counter was empty, and his stomach grumbled. Even bad hotels offered a few free bagels in the morning.

"We'll get you a zero-gravity granola bar," said

Sam. "They found our ship."

Neil's eyebrows arched in surprise, and he turned toward Dallas, his eyes finally adjusting to the crisp LED lighting.

"The *Newt* is hiding in a pile of floating junk. Whoever it is that hacked our whole system did the same to all our online satellites, and they figured they wouldn't be seen," explained Dallas to her group of tired recruits.

"But they forgot about one, the Hubble. The space telescope had a camera installed years ago that transmitted photos back over a dedicated fax line."

"What's a 'fax'?" asked Biggs.

"It's a facsimile transmission device. Old-school. It's how we received this." Dallas held up a piece of paper, which showed a blurry, pixelated patch of debris. "Right *there* is the *Newt*," she said, pointing to a glob of black ink with the tip of a red pen. It barely looked like anything, let alone a top-of-the-line spacecraft. "Now it's time to go get it."

"And save the planet?" asked Neil, recalling what Finch had told him. He remembered Sam's weird feeling about the mission. He was starting to get the same impression . . . something was wrong.

The Chief CAPCOM cocked her head curiously.

"Finch told me everything," said Neil, making sure the rest of the group was out of earshot.

He was really getting the hang of the whole lying thing.

"I see," Dallas said, her forehead wrinkling. "Well, Finch is putting the final touches on the mission, and he'll update you at the launch pad."

"Plan 'Zee," said Neil.

"Right. So you know the ultimate threat that Q-94 poses."

"Yes. I do," Neil said. Q-94 was the name of a local radio station playing hits from forgotten decades, but apparently it was also the name of a world-destroying threat.

"The Q-94 might be the most dangerous asteroid that's ever headed toward Earth, but we'll be with you the whole mission."

Neil did a double take. Did Dallas just say *asteroid*?

★ ★ ★

Neil and his crew huddled together in a huge industrial elevator leading to the *Fossil*. Commander Finch stood in the center, a foot taller than the ragtag crew surrounding him.

People talked, but *asteroid* was the only word in Neil's head.

"As I assume Dallas briefed you all, we've found the orbital path of our missing ship, the *Newt*," Finch said, clutching a clipboard in his hands. "Weather conditions are currently perfect for a launch, so the mission must start immediately."

"What's going on, Commander?" asked Sam.

"With the intel from that photo, we've mapped the orbit of the ship. As of the last transmitted photograph, it hasn't moved, so we'll be able to send the *Fossil* on a course to intercept."

"That's nice. But what's going on with Q-94?" Neil said bluntly. He couldn't help it.

Finch's face remained calm.

"I see Dallas has briefed you all," the commander said.

"Something like that," Neil replied.

"Well, it's best you all know anyways," Finch started. "For a few years now, we've been following and tracking near-Earth objects massive enough to pose a threat to our planet. Our attention was drawn to an asteroid. Q-94. At its current velocity and angle, it is due to collide with Earth."

Neil felt a little light-headed. The group was silent.

"We've been hoping that its collision course would alter, but it's headed directly for our planet. NASA has been preparing the fleet of Whiptails in case we need to face the worst. Fortunately we still have time. By our calculations, the asteroid will collide in two weeks. But the *Newt* is our last chance at stopping the asteroid before it gets too close. That's why it is so valuable to us."

"Why doesn't everybody know about this?" asked a concerned JP. "This type of thing should be public knowledge."

Neil agreed. Even if they couldn't stop it, people at least deserved to know there was precious little time to secure high scores in favorite games.

"By the way, great questions, everyone. I'm very proud," Finch said, in a giddy, geeked-out way. "Yes, people should know, but it's a tricky balance. We always want to solve the problem without inciting panic. That's why getting the *Newt* back is our top priority."

"We can do it, sir," said Trevor, catching everyone a bit off guard. "You can count on us."

Others nodded in support. While Neil was surprised to hear Trevor be so positive, he did agree wholeheartedly.

If he and his friends were the only people able to get this ship back, well, then they had to. And if a kid like Trevor was being heroic, backing out would look pretty bad.

"Now if you'll bear with me, I'm going to dole out crew positions. I'd hoped to have more time to run simulations with all of you and not base your talents off a written exam, but it is what it is." He scribbled a few more words down on the clipboard in his hands.

"Payload specialists will be Waffles and Dale. Guys, you'll be in charge of the auxiliary features of the ship, like the pulse cannon to disable the *Newt*. And anything that blows up."

"Awesome," said the twin brothers in unison.

Finch read on, his voice exuberantly bouncing up and down in pitch. Neil thought he sounded like his dad before a days-long camping adventure. They seemed to share the same zest for trips to locations without running water.

"Medical specialists are Sam and . . . well, Sam, you'll be alone. Your scores were off the charts. JP, you'll be in charge of radar. Most of our electronics have a few lingering bugs from whatever the space thieves have done, but it should work."

Finch kept reading the list of new positions.

"On consumables will be Riley and Corinne. There should be enough dehydrated food for two weeks on board, so food shouldn't be an issue. Plus the ship's made to launch carrying enough bananas for twelve chimpanzees, so you'll be loaded up.

"Hurbigg, you'll be our communications specialist. You'll be the point of contact with the mission CAPCOM, Dallas."

Neil couldn't help but feel that putting Biggs in charge of communication was dangerous. At the very least, he would set a record for the most times *dude* was said over official NASA airwaves.

"Now for pilots and deputy pilots," Finch said as Neil's heart began to thump. "Jason 1 and Jason 2, from what Dallas has told me about your simulation, you'll be my deputies. We'll need both of you ready to fly back in our stolen bird."

The two high-fived gloved hands.

"And at the top of the chain of command will be Andertol and Grunsten," Finch explained. "They'll report to me, and all of you will report to them."

Neil wished he had enough time to explain to Finch

how awful an idea giving Trevor power would be, and how he'd probably make everyone watch him do fencing exercises. But the commander was all business, and he didn't allow for a word edgewise.

"Your next-generation Whiptail, like I said, should be bug-free," Finch said. "Since I won't be in the ship with you, I'll need to be alerted of any issues. We've got one shot. One shot to make it count. Let's make it successful."

Neil felt the seriousness of the moment. It was like a hot wave quickly washing over him. The subtle whirring of the elevator heaving them upward was still constant.

"So if you're not coming with us, who is commander? What are we supposed to do?" asked Trevor, his voice sharp and demanding. Neil could sense Trevor was vying to be selected.

"I'm no longer cleared for flight. During a space walk a few years ago, I had to save a satellite from drifting into orbit. Held on to the shuttle with my left hand and grabbed the thing with my free hand," Finch said, demonstrating with an intense clenched fist. "Tore basically everything in my right shoulder. Now my body can't withstand the g forces associated with space travel. Plus I can't fit in that spaceship; I'll feel like I'm in a dollhouse."

Finch took two steps toward the lift's doors, spinning to face all eleven gamers-turned-Air-Force-pilots-turned-astronauts. He placed a hand on Neil's shoulder.

"But, Andertol, I believe you've got what it takes to lead this crew," Finch said confidently.

Neil could feel sweat building on his palms as his throat slowly began to close.

"From what I've seen, and what Jones has told me, you're the person for the job," Finch said to Neil before pivoting his head to the group. "You know, at first I didn't know if this would work, but I've got faith in you. In all of you."

"Hail Lord Commander Andertol!" shouted Riley. "May he be a fair and wise dictator! A friend to man and beast, particularly hogs and their overseers!"

"Well, I don't know about that part, but sounds good to me," said Sam. "Just know we're counting on you, ManofNeil."

This seemed to be the final opportunity to come clean, to let Finch and the group know how Neil had stretched the truth. How he had a maximum of forty minutes logged in Shuttle Fury, which included bathroom breaks.

--

"If I had any doubt in Neil, the mission wouldn't happen," eased Finch. "Now, we've got minutes until takeoff. We'll be in constant radio contact. I'll be with you the whole way, as well as the astronaut flying with you in the middeck."

"An astronaut? I thought you said nobody could fit in the *Fossil*?" asked a befuddled Neil.

"Correct, but there's a retired Russian cosmonaut we're bringing in to fly with you. He'll handle the technical aspects of flight. He's trained for monitoring pressurization and fuel levels," said Finch as the hulking elevator came to a stop. The doors opened to a cream-colored spaceship.

Waiting for them on the bridge was a chimpanzee in a green-and-white jumpsuit, his name stitched onto it in bright-red cursive lettering. He had a wrinkled, agitated face complete with a small scar on his left cheek. Gray hair framed his face. He looked at Neil and the others and spit on the metal floor of the walkway.

"Recruits, meet Boris."

CHAPTER

11

INSIDE THE *FOSSIL*, THEY WERE FORCED TO CROUCH AS THEY made their way to the cramped main flight cabin. White space suits with helmets and backpacks full of oxygen were secured to the walls.

The whole craft itself was a small compact wedge, like a space shuttle and a minivan merged together. It had stubby wings that stuck out on either side and four windows looking out from the control deck. At any given time, Neil was basically touching two of his fellow recruits, and everything pretty much smelled like a zoo exhibit.

"Now just know we'll be with you the whole time. We'll be in constant contact during the entire mission," said Finch. "Everyone settled in?"

Everyone gave him a thumbs-up, and Neil could hear the exterior door of the ship being sealed. Dale closed the circular door leading from the ship's main cabin into the air lock. He latched it shut with a firm twist of the metal handle and then secured himself into his locking chair.

There were two rows of seats separated by a small space to walk in the center. Dale and Waffles were seated way in the back, with Neil and Trevor up front. Sam was behind Trevor, and the seat behind her was left empty, meant for Yuri. Jason 1 and Jason 2 completed the row ending with Waffles's grinning face.

Across the small primate walkway, and directly behind Neil, was JP. Then Biggs, in charge of communicating with Dallas, and Riley and Corinne took the seats after.

Neil looked at the control panels in front of him. All things considered, it looked rather familiar. The gauges seemed similar enough to the ones Chameleons had, and the joystick for the Whiptail felt comfortable in Neil's hands. It felt like the whole thing was created to be like a video game, just designed for chimpanzees. Controls and gauges used pictures instead of words. A few were marked with pictures of apes screaming, with red circles slashed through them.

"Okay, I won't touch some of those controls. Whatever they may be," Neil said to himself.

With a howl, Boris descended to the middeck, below the flight deck. A hatch in the floor led to his boiler room–like quarters, where he was to regulate the pressurization and other technical aspects of the flight.

"Come in, Biggs. Repeat, come in, Biggs. Do you hear me?" said a voice over the headset pulled over each gamer's head. It was Dallas.

"Read you loud and clear, Houston," Biggs said. "Er, Dallas. Someplace in Texas. Listen, we've got an angry-chimpanzee situation happening. Any advice on how to approach it?"

"Don't worry about him; he's always cranky," said Dallas through the ship's radio. Everybody could hear both sides of the conversation, but only Biggs had actual radio control. "That's why he had to leave his crew and come retire in Florida. They couldn't take it anymore. Boris, are you clear for launch?"

The chimpanzee underfoot gave a couple of quick whimpers followed by a metallic clanking noise.

"Copy that. You're all set for launch, recruits."

"Well, that sounds promising," said Sam from her seat.

Neil shifted in the tiny pilot's perch. Under an insulated white space suit, Neil wore a thin heating and cooling unit that channeled water through every inch of an astronaut's constricting pressure suit. It was a bit stiff, but Neil had a feeling it could come in handy.

He twisted his neck to let a little air flow past his sweaty neck.

"Let's see if your Chameleon skills carry over into the space race," said Trevor as he and Neil watched the launch timer slowly count down from sixty. They checked gauges on liquid oxygen and hydrogen, but mostly prepared themselves for g forces that might squeeze all liquids from their bodies. Boris would be able to adjust any levels—they could simply focus on flying the craft once it reached outer space.

The rocket would propel the capsule and the Whiptail spacecraft to the farthest reaches of Earth's atmosphere.

The main boosters would detach, and the Whiptail's jet engine would take over. Neil could hear the bridge and scaffolding pull away. For now the windows were still dark and covered.

"Ten . . ." came Dallas's voice over the ship's radio.

"Well, I feel great about Neil being in control," said Biggs from his station. He made a signal with his hand that kind of looked like a rabbit with four or five legs. The Universal Biggs Language was going to need a pretty thorough reference key to clear up any confusion.

"Nine . . ."

"Eight . . ."

Neil nodded his head, and Finch's voice filled the helmet of every suit.

"Okay, astronauts. Just like your last mission," Finch said as the final seconds ticked by with robotic beeping noises. "And don't think I'm not timing this. Extra points for a speedy recovery."

Neil gave himself a few seconds to breathe, and with that, the microphoned voice of Finch declared liftoff.

Neil felt a low rumble, unlike anything he'd experienced before. The rocket violently shimmied back and forth and was suddenly plucked up from the ground. It was like someone dropped a yo-yo, only to jerk it back up toward their palm in an instant.

The unrelenting power of five gs of pressure crushed Neil as the ship rocketed toward space.

But then Neil felt a slight change in trajectory. He heard a bleating warning noise coming from his control dashboard.

While the initial thrust felt like the rocket was headed straight up, it now felt like they were jetting through the atmosphere at a weird angle. The plane was veering downward.

Summoning all his strength, Neil asked a question of his deputy pilot, Jason 1.

"What's . . . our . . . altitude?" Neil said, forcing his body to use neck muscles he didn't even know existed.

"We've not yet broken the atmosphere," Jason 1 responded.

If the rocket were off by the slightest bit, they would come crashing back to Earth in a few deadly seconds.

As his body was jostled with the force of ten rickety traveling-carnival rides, Neil's eyes turned to the manual override.

There was no other choice. Neil disengaged the auto-pilot and took control of the spacecraft. The controls felt sort of like a Chameleon, and Neil manipulated the ship with confidence.

"What are you doing?" croaked Trevor from the seat next to Neil.

"Keeping us alive," Neil said as the spaceplane burst out of the payload capsule protecting it. As the nose of the plane cleared the debris, Neil was greeted by a blinding light.

"Oh man! Aliens!" Biggs yelled.

"No, snow!" shouted Neil as he wrestled with the craft's controls. For a split second the flurries of snow opened up, and Neil watched a jagged mountain range appear before him, like the teeth of an angry snow monster.

Neil yanked the controls left, but the speed of the *Fossil* was too much, and the ship designed to explore galaxies collided with an arctic mountain range. The crew screamed as the thud of the crash resonated up through the seats they were strapped into.

Neil looked for any lever or handle marked with a flying chimp and pulled them all furiously. He could feel the ship at the edge of a cliff, just barely, come to a complete stop. A glaringly white expanse stretched before them.

"Welcome to space, you guys!" shouted Waffles.

CHAPTER

12

NEIL GROANED AS HE UNFASTENED HIMSELF FROM THE SEAT to make sure each body part was still intact. They were, barely.

"So, what now? Unless the universe looks like a ski resort, I'd say we're in the wrong place," said Corinne, worried.

"And I think the crash broke the radio. I can't hear NASA anymore," said Biggs. "Hello? Houston? Dallas?"

A transmission fuzzed in and out, but it was mainly clipped words and choppy noises.

"We must be near a magnetic pole. There's a field of something interfering," said JP, inspecting the waveform transmitted by the radio. "Hello? Houston, are you there?" Only a static buzz answered him.

"Well, I'm not just sitting here," said Sam as she unhooked herself from her chair.

The eleven crew members filed out of the door Finch sealed minutes before, squinting at the snowy wilderness around them. They all wore their compressed NASA flight suits, clear helmets firmly attached to their uniforms. Since they were not yet in space, the bulkier suits meant for space walking stayed tied to the walls of the air lock. Snow flew diagonally, and powder whipped up off the ground in all directions. Visibility was an issue, as anything past twenty yards was a white blurry mess.

"Well, what's the plan, dude who got put in charge?" asked Waffles. They all turned to Neil, the commander and leader of their now-arctic adventure.

"Yes, Master and Commander, where are we?" said Riley. "Our town blacksmith, Lord Carl, tells horrific tales of cannibal Vikings and frost ogres in places such as these."

Frigid winds swept up all around the crew, relentlessly pummeling the side of the ship, which echoed through the mountain range with a spooky howl.

Neil felt pressured to provide answers. He looked to Sam for assistance, but her face seemed as scared and concerned as the others'.

"Well, first things first, let's look at the plane for any damage," Neil said.

Hey, that actually sounded like the correct thing to do.

"Right," said Dale, followed by his brother.

The team quickly spread out around the now-frostbitten Whiptail, stamping about until they found a small spot of damage on the wing.

A tiny corner of a piece of the high-tech paneling had peeled up, barely a malfunction but enough to alter the course of the ship.

Trevor kicked a huge chunk of snow in front of him and thrashed his arms in frustration.

"Well, now what do we do out here, huh?" Trevor screamed, his visible breath getting shorter and more frequent.

A few people moaned, and nobody seemed ready to refute Trevor. Without any way to get ahold of Finch or NASA, being stranded was becoming a distinct possibility.

"Well, let's not overreact," Neil said, half in agreement

with Trevor's negative outlook.

Trevor kicked the metallic side of the plane's wing. The space-age material absorbed the kick, but Neil watched some snow from the collision fall from the ship's wing. A small logo was uncovered on the corner of the heavily bolted metal sheeting.

BEED INDUSTRIES it read, with some sort of long lightning bolt in the background.

Neil crinkled his eyebrows—that name sounded familiar.

Harris Beed! Beed Industries belonged to Harris's father!

"Guys. If we can't reach NASA," Neil said, the gears of his brain turning, "maybe we can get . . . Harris."

"You mean the guy who basically tried to illegally steal a top secret jet, as well as destroy all video games in the world apart from his own?" JP asked, his voice serious and concerned.

"Yup, that's the one," Neil said, his voice brimming with confidence. "In case you guys have forgotten, we have a mission to get back to, a ship to fix, one to save, and right now Harris's help is our only option."

He knew Harris wasn't actually an awful person, just a bit mixed up. If anyone was able to help them out in a ridiculous situation like this, it would be Harris, a ridiculous person.

"Now we just need to figure out a way to contact him. Our radios are definitely out?"

"Yes, Commander. Maybe something just got knocked loose," said JP, heading back inside the *Fossil*.

"I could go check on it, too. But I'm not exactly sure how it all works," said Trevor. "I can't figure out if a chimpanzee picture with a mouth closed and arms straight up means 'do' or 'do not touch.'"

"Okay. Biggs and the twins stay with me. Everyone else head inside; we're going to go find some help. You said you've been working with Harris, right?" Neil asked. "We need to find a way to call him."

The rest of the group trudged inside. Sam gave Neil a hug and sent them off.

"I've got Harris's private number," Biggs said proudly. "We've been trying to find a time to talk about some new smells for our game. He's a very particular man when it comes to his privacy and ostrich scents."

Neil felt weirdly jealous. After exchanging gaming names earlier, he had expected to be the one hearing from Harris.

- -

"Let's find a lookout," said a helpful Dale.

With squeaks from their bulky space-suit boots, Waffles and Dale attempted to scramble up the ship's wing to climb to the top. The snowy conditions didn't help matters, and the two kept sliding back down. They trudged through the snow to the front of the plane, and Biggs boosted the brothers up. Neil followed behind, resting a hand on the side of the spaceship.

"You know, call me crazy, but I might know this mountain range," said Waffles, glaring out across ice fields sparkling in the fierce sunbeams. "Yeah, I think if we just curl around that last hill, there may be something. I kind of think this is a level on Yeti Bobsled."

"You think? Also, what's Yeti Bobsled?" asked Neil. He'd spent all summer glued to Chameleon, so he wasn't up-to-date on the newest offerings in the gaming world.

"It's sort of like hide-and-seek with mythical frost beasts," Waffles explained. "It's a five, maybe six, out of ten. Could use more yetis. But this mountain range is definitely in there. I remember that hill that looks like a baby camel. There's an outpost that way. Can you see a beacon?"

Neil thought for a second, following Waffles's pointed

finger toward a small humped mountain with a speck of blue light. It was a better plan than nothing.

"Guess we've got no other choice. Let's go, everybody. Waffles, we'll follow your lead," Neil said. As commander of the mission, Neil knew he had to make decisions, and fast. Now, just how were they going to get there?

"I'll come with you guys," added Biggs.

The brothers climbed down from the ship, and Dale ducked inside the chimp-scented air lock of the *Fossil*. He quickly reappeared, and in his arms he clutched a yellow plastic brick. Neil instantly recognized it as an inflatable emergency raft. It looked just like the one from the Chameleon. The twin brothers pulled a valve, and the raft sprang to life.

"I think this might work," said Waffles, looking at the steep hillside around him. While the *Fossil* was angled directly off an icy cliff, the other side of the peak was a gradual decline that fed into a snowy valley. It looked like a ski resort's quadruple-black-diamond run.

Biggs hopped into the raft and grabbed tightly onto one of the canvas straps stemming from the floor. Dale stood behind and braced both hands on the back of the emergency blow-up sled.

"A yeti bobsled isn't complete without four people," said Waffles, trying to wedge himself into the raft. "Technically it's not complete without three hundred pounds of yak meat, but we'll make do. Now hop in!"

Well, here goes nothing.

Neil jumped into the inflatable life raft, and Dale gave them all a quick push before darting in next to his brother. They instantly gained speed. They coasted over snow and ice, leaving a trail of flurries in their wake.

CHAPTER

13

COMMANDER ANDERTOL AND HIS CREW FINALLY ARRIVED
at the arctic outpost.

Pale-yellow sunlight illuminated the shack. It was
just bigger than a semi, with a blue light flashing on top
of a pole.

Up a tiny stairway was a door and a small window.

"Hello? Anyone?" Neil said as he opened the door.
The station was a big open room, with papers messily
strewn about over tables and laboratory equipment. Low
static warbled over a radio telecom system. It looked

deserted, but Neil soon saw what they'd come for: a telephone.

"Biggs," Neil said, tipping his head toward the phone.

"On it, my good man," Biggs said, confirming with a new piece of sign language that involved lots of finger twisting.

"I'm gonna try and call NASA first," Biggs said, bringing the old brown phone to his ear. He cocked his head to the side to pinch the receiver between his shoulder and his cheek. "You think it's just 1-800-NASA?"

Biggs smashed the number into the keypad and soon heard a busy signal. He called again, this time getting through for a ring, but then he only received a recorded message about early registration for Space Camp.

"No luck," said Biggs as he hung up the phone. Neil, Dale, and Waffles had all continued riffling through papers, which seemed to be in both English and Russian.

Biggs dialed another number and held an arm high with a thumbs-up as it successfully started to ring.

"Whoa, jackpot!" yelled Dale as he opened a small refrigerator in the corner of the room. He pulled out cans of Coke and tossed one to each fellow adventurer. Neil popped the top of his drink and listened intently to Biggs. He glanced over to the flimsy wooden door on the other side of the room and took a quick gulp of his drink. The fizzing bubbles tickled his throat.

"Are you there, Harris? It's me, Biggs," Neil's friend said, twisting the phone cord around his index finger. "First, great news on the smell front. I think we're close to working those kinks out. Which is to say, about only half of the stuff still smells like dirty wildlife."

Neil cleared his throat, respectfully reminding Biggs of the task at hand.

"Oh, right," Biggs continued. "And more important, Neil, you remember Neil, right? Well, we're actually flying a plane made by your father's company."

Biggs continued on, explaining as much as he could. Waffles then ran up to him, excitedly pointing to a map with specifics on their location.

Neil knew Harris was their only chance, and Harris needed to understand how serious the situation was. Neil walked over to Biggs and motioned for the phone before plucking it from Biggs's hand.

"Harris, I hate to be demanding, but I could really

use a favor right about now. We have to fix this spaceship and get back to our mission," Neil begged. *"Please*, come help us."

Neil started to hear a voice on the other line, but the connection cut out.

Well, better than nothing.

"Uh, guys?" said Waffles, moving into his friends while purposefully backing away from the door.

Commotion sounded from outside. A crash was followed by a menacing growl. *What was that, a yeti? Santa?*

It was, in fact, a polar bear. And it was blocking the door they had just come through.

"Run!" Neil screamed as the group bolted out the door on the other side of the building. It might as well have been marked "Polar Bear Escape Route."

"So how do we outrun a polar bear? Is that in the game?" Neil wheezed, turning to Dale. They watched the wild animal race toward them across the snow.

"I have no idea!" Dale exclaimed. "Truth be told, Yeti Bobsled got pulled from the shelves for overly realistic Abominable Snowman violence. Every game ended with some kind of snow monster using your femur as a toothpick."

"Why didn't we hear about this before sledding down a mountain?" yelled Neil. The bear had followed them outside and was in pursuit.

Neil was panicked, and he knew he had to do something. The bear was right on their heels when Neil remembered his hand was still clutching a can of Coca-Cola. And based on his extensive television watching, Neil knew that polar bears *loved* Coca-Cola.

He turned and faced the bear, which reared up on its hind legs and growled dangerously, strands of saliva dangling from its sharp teeth.

"I hope this works," Neil gulped. Waving the can of Coke like a stick in a game of fetch, he hurled it as hard as he possibly could. Neil had hoped to throw it beyond the bear so the bear would chase after it. Instead, the half-full can spiraled wildly, exploding in a shower of carbonated, sugary goodness.

Neil closed his eyes in terror, sure that the bear had a taste for sugar and that it was smelling the Swedish fish coursing through his veins. But as his breath fogged up against his clear helmet, Neil opened his eyes to see nothing had happened.

The bear was on all fours, licking at the Coke that

had landed in the snow. It was like a Coke slushy, and Neil appreciated the bear for its good taste. Neil would do the same with his friend Tyler, eating syrup-stained chunks of snow one snowball at a time.

"Come on, guys!" Neil said. The bear was certainly under some sort of sugar-high trance, so they had to move fast.

Neil, Biggs, Waffles, and Dale followed their snowy footprints from earlier and dragged the inflatable raft behind them. It seemed impossible to move fast, though. Sliding downhill was a breeze, but climbing back up was proving impossible.

Neil and the others stopped, panting. They had made it maybe ten meters before doubling over, out of breath.

"Man, we didn't really think about how we were gonna get back up this thing," said a tired Waffles. But as everyone looked up the imposing face of the jagged mountain, Neil heard a voice behind him.

"You called for help?"

CHAPTER 14

"HARRIS!" SHOUTED NEIL, IN TOTAL SHOCK.

He was wearing full puffy winter wear, riding on an ostrich decked out in a furry insulated vest and ski goggles. They both wore Feather Duster–branded gear, everything light blue apart from a yellow ostrich symbol.

"Did you guys miss me?" he said, pulling his orange snow goggles down around his neck. His skin was still dark from the sun, the remnants of a few recent pimples dotting his forehead. He had the same piercing eyes Neil remembered, but this time they didn't seem evil. Neil had to admit Harris had a pretty intimidating and confident presence.

"How'd you get here so fast?" shouted Biggs.

Harris dismounted from his winter ostrich, which crunched at the snow with insulated boots with holes for talons. He began collecting a few of the canvas tethers attached to the raft.

"So wild," Harris said, taking off a white helmet that looked like the kind professional snowboarders wore. "I'm up north doing research for *Feather Duster 3: Aviary Avalanche*. My dad's company has an outpost not far from here."

"Oh, we got the full tour, my man," replied Waffles.

"Oof, yeah," Harris said. He began rigging his ostrich to the yellow sled. "Been abandoned for a bit. It's Fuzzy's home now. He was my old pet, but he started getting too big for his cage. So he lives here. I think he likes it."

As the caretaker of a backyard ostrich, Neil saw an alarming trend with Harris and his pets. Unfortunately Neil's family didn't have some kind of subzero outpost to which they could ship away an overgrown bird.

"Well, that should about do it," said Harris, tugging

on the harness he'd just created. "You guys hop on. We're following the trail you left coming down, I assume?"

"You've got it," said Neil. He was relieved to see Harris, but more excited that he no longer had to trudge back up the mountain. Harris nudged his ostrich, and they began heading uphill.

"Biggs, how're the smells for the game going?" Harris continued.

"We're, ah, getting there," said Biggs. "I've got a few scents I'm cooking up in some jars back home. Really think I've figured out how to get rid of 'wet dog.'"

The crew soon went silent, hunkering down to dodge snowdrifts. Harris and his ostrich finally lugged the group back to the *Fossil*. Everybody was inside, but Neil could see Riley and Corinne waving through the cockpit windows.

Everyone filed back outside in the swirling cold winds, and Harris's eye caught sight of the damaged wing.

"That the problem?" Harris asked as he walked over to the wing, leaving his ostrich to peck at big clumps of snow. He stooped down and ran a gloved hand over the small corner of sheeting.

"Ah, I see," Harris said calmly, pulling out a tool kit from the ostrich saddle.

"See what?" said Biggs.

"I know we were having issues with some of the spacecraft paneling as it came off the line. Could've been what happened here," Harris said, pulling out what looked like a shiny blowtorch. "But we can fix this. No problem."

Neil could sense some of the group was hesitant about having a former evil lunatic helping them out.

"Are we sure we can trust him?" Sam whispered to Neil.

"What choice do we have?" Neil mumbled back, taking a wide-legged stance that hopefully made him look bigger than he was. "Harris, do your best."

With a nod, Harris sparked the handheld welder and began repairs to the ship.

"So, mind telling me what, exactly, you're all doing up here?" Harris said, closing his eyes to avoid the blue spark of his torch.

Neil told Harris about the mission. How they'd been selected to retrieve a stolen spaceship. Neil chuckled as he wondered what was more random, the mission he'd just described or the fact that Harris rolled around with a spot welder at all times.

"Okay, this should do it," Harris said after a couple of minutes.

"Thanks," Neil said. "You've literally saved this whole mission."

Neil opened his arms for a hug good-bye, but Harris took a step forward and lowered Neil's arms back down to his sides for him.

"Nope, I'm coming with you," Harris said.

Neil laughed, but as Harris began to leave behind his winter gear in his ostrich saddle, he could see the face of someone who'd made up his mind.

"Really," he insisted, determined. "I owe you guys from last time. And I love a good mission. Who doesn't?"

"It'll be dangerous," Neil replied, but Harris was unflinching. "We're basically chasing someone who has hacked an entire government branch."

"Only one?" he said to Neil, taking his snow-caked scarf off his neck. "Neil, I'm coming. I've done four flights with my dad and his pet space project, Beed-X. We've been making supply runs to the ISS for months now."

Neil had heard about private companies doing flights to the International Space Station. It made sense Harris's billionaire father was getting into the mix.

"And besides, there's normally twelve of you, right? From my count I only saw eleven."

Man, this guy is good.

"Yeah," Neil said. "Yuri didn't make the mission. You might remember him as the dude who smashed that huge window in your dad's old warehouse."

Harris bobbed his head in acknowledgment.

"Fine. You can be the engineering specialist on board, in case anything else breaks," said Sam, reluctantly welcoming her newest teammate.

"Well, what are you?" Harris asked her.

"Medical specialist. Basically I just slap anti-nausea patches on people who look like they're going to hurl."

"I'll take one of those. And we're in luck if you need backup; my CPR card is up to date, and I've seen the first three seasons of the reality TV hit *My Big Fat Rural Disaster.*"

"Well, welcome aboard, Astronaut Beed," Neil said with a salute.

Harris gave a salute with two fingers and, with a

whistle, sent his ostrich running home. He followed Neil into the main flight cabin containing all twelve seats, Neil's up front next to Trevor's.

"Here's the only spare space suit we have," said Jason 1, holding out a vintage burned-orange suit. As it was designed for a chimpanzee, it was a little long in the arms and short in the legs, but Harris could make do. The name *Pickles* was printed on its front in block letters.

"I know some of you may not be excited to see me, but I want to help you guys out. To do what I can to make up for last time," Harris said as everyone began reattaching their seat belts and fastening them in place. "Oh, and one more thing."

All eleven gamers went silent, wondering if this was when Harris would unleash a thousand ostriches to overthrow the mission and NASA as a whole.

"We're going to need to fly off the cliff."

"What?" everyone exclaimed.

"Listen, I know it sounds crazy, but trust me," Harris explained. "I did something similar with my dad during one of his commercial flights."

"Like a TV commercial?" asked Jason 2.

"No, the private company Beed-X. He's trying to be

the first private team that makes it into deep space."

"Lucky," said Sam.

"My dad showed me all the specs for these things. The engine on this ship was probably designed to work like a booster rocket, right?"

"Correct," said JP from his seat.

"So for the thrusters to work properly on this thing, we really need to be moving," Harris said. Neil could tell he had a take-charge personality—perfect for unexpected problems on top secret missions, horrible for board games.

"So in order to take off, we, well . . . ," Harris said, trailing off.

"We'll have to free-fall from the cliff for a minimum of eight seconds. It's a three-hundred-foot drop, so we *should* be okay," JP said, interrupting. "By my calculations."

Neil was beginning to get slimy palms. The pressure of commanding the ship and mission, without radio support, was mounting. He could feel more eyes looking his way for direction.

Am I really about to give this order?

"Crew, you've received the orders," Neil said in his

best Jones impersonation. "Now let's get a move on it. Fasten yourselves in and prepare for takeoff. On my mark, we'll disengage our flaps and, ah, fly off the cliff, I guess."

While the speech probably wasn't up to his standard, Neil hoped Jones would be proud. Maybe there were some freeze-dried sunflower seeds on board, to make his impersonation complete.

Neil put a hand on the flap controls.

"Everyone ready?" Neil asked his team, and himself.

"Let's do this, baby!" shouted Waffles.

"We'll follow your lead, my liege! We've got a mission to finish! The cosmos calls us!" added Riley.

At the edge of the frozen ice cliff, the craft creaked on tightly packed snow.

Terrified, Neil pulled the handle. The flaps of the ship lifted up, and the rocket instantly slipped forward, careening off the lip of the cliff.

It fell faster and faster toward the ground, building speed as it tore through the cold arctic air. Trevor was counting down from eight.

"Four . . . three . . . two . . . ," he said through everyone's radio communication.

"The engine isn't catching!" JP shouted, frantically

checking every gauge and control in front of him.

"We can't die like this!" shouted Corinne. "My body is supposed to be turned into ashes, then converted into pages for encyclopedias!"

But in the final second, the engine of the ship fired a glowing red and blue. JP shot the ship forward, and Neil and Trevor pulled hard to guide the nose upward. With force that was five times that of a Chameleon, Neil and his crew launched forward. Everyone held on tightly as the rumbling ship soared up, up, up.

CHAPTER

15

NEIL CLOSED HIS EYES AS HE FELT THE G FORCES PUSHING down on him. He tried to focus on more tricks to breathing steadily, but his mind could only think of things that could go wrong. There were quite a few of them.

Were they headed in the right direction? Had Harris properly fixed the wing? Was Biggs currently answering nature's call in his suit?

Neil's body was filled with a sensation of complete lightness.

"*Sch . . . chh . . .* recruits?" buzzed the radio. It was

Dallas's voice, coming through in fuzzy clipped waves.

"We're here, Houston-Dallas! We made it!" said Biggs through his radio headset. "Dallas?"

Only crackling and the occasional high-pitched squeak came through the radio.

"Still must be something wrong," said JP. "But I think I've fixed the radar, at least."

Neil looked out of the cockpit windows to the blue atmosphere of Earth, which slowly gave way to an intimidating blackness. Neil was speechless. His body was strapped into the tiny primate-sized chair, but Neil could feel himself bobbing in the half inch of wiggle room.

This is amazing.

This wasn't just floating in a fake air hockey simulation; this was real. It made flying a Chameleon feel like riding a bike with training wheels. Really, really awesome training wheels, but restricted nonetheless.

Automatically, the ship's engine decreased its thrust. It glided as if sliding on ice, responding to any minor piloting correction. The *Fossil* slowly twisted, and the blue orb of Earth appeared in the small cockpit windows of the ship.

All twelve astronauts were stunned, and only the

hum of the ship's computers and oxygen filtration filled the cabin. There was also the occasional chimpanzee shriek from the deck below, but Boris seemed to pretty much keep to himself otherwise.

It almost looked fake, Earth. Like something Finch would've projected back in the NASA training room. White clouds swirled over choppy oceans and coastlines covered in greenery. Islands in blue water looked like floating pieces of cereal. Neil wasn't prepared for how huge the planet would look.

"Whoa, you can see satellites," said Jason 2. "I wonder how many channels we could get up here."

Neil watched the tiny metal structures suspended in orbit. His eyes also caught the glint of smaller objects dangling precariously above Earth.

"Space junk," JP said, referring to a silvery ribbon of old broken satellite equipment.

"Think there's a space recycling program, Biggs?" said Neil. He chuckled at his joke, but it didn't get as big a response from his conservationist friend as he'd hoped.

"Why should I know?" Biggs said defensively.

"Whoa, sorry, man. Just thought, you know, you'd

be interested," Neil replied. "Because of recycling? How it's kind of your thing?"

"No, I'm sorry. That was a bit harsh," Biggs said. "But you did just grab that phone from my hand in the polar bear den before I could finish explaining everything to Harris—that's all."

"What? A polar bear den?" asked Jason 1. "And we missed that!"

"Oh," Neil said. He didn't enjoy this new feeling of weirdness between him and Biggs, but he didn't apologize. As commander, he did need to make sure everything was done, and done properly. He was just taking charge.

"Trouble in Bromance Town," said Sam. Harris, in the chair behind her, laughed along with his new crew—maybe even a bit too hard.

"No, no trouble," Biggs reassured. "Bromance Town is thriving. The mayor's doing some great work there."

Neil smirked, and his eyes wandered to the pulsing, pristine stars spread out in every direction. As the now-blindingly bright sun dipped behind Earth, Neil felt the immensity of the universe around him. The shimmering darkness of space was awe-inspiring, and it sort of looked like the dark velvet material from the pants his grandmother always wore to brunch.

"Recruits!" said Dallas's voice, clear for the moment. "Think . . . communication . . ."

"What's that, Dallas? Repeat, please?" said Biggs.

"We . . . can't talk . . . with our shuttle. Only hours . . . but the *Newt*! You must get the *Newt* . . . coordinates."

On JP's radar screen, a long series of numbers appeared.

"Yes! The coordinates NASA received from the Hubble telescope," said JP. "It's where Dallas said we can find the *Newt*. And it's not far from here."

The radio transmission fizzled, and Biggs frantically pushed buttons to try and bring it back. He flipped a switch that had two bananas on it. Nothing happened, so he flipped a switch picturing three bananas. Still nothing.

"Dallas? Did we lose you again?" said Biggs.

A big wave of space junk floated past.

"Let's move out of this stuff. JP, enter those coordinates. Full speed ahead," said Commander Andertol to his crew. It was tough to see through the flurry of spiraling space garbage, but Neil's eyes stayed fixed on open spaces for maneuvering.

- -

"Hold on, everybody." Neil grabbed what he thought was the throttle, making the ship spin in an erratic circle.

"What are you doing, Neil?" yelled Trevor.

"Whoops, sorry about that," said Neil.

Even with minimal training on Shuttle Fury, Neil was able to fly mostly on instinct.

Neil composed himself and pulled the ship out of a spiral. The joystick in his control felt exactly like a video game's. He didn't need to know scientific words or the actual physics assisting him in the miracle of flight—this spaceship did everything Neil wanted it to do.

The *Fossil* finally reached the coordinates provided by NASA.

"I don't see anything," said Trevor, leaning forward in his harness to get a better view. His head darted up and down as he tried to look out at every possible angle.

Just as another passing mess of satellite shreds coasted out of view, the ship's radar began a steady beep. The noises grew faster and louder as Neil saw a blue spark. It was the back of the *Newt*.

CHAPTER

16

BETWEEN PIECES OF SPIRALING METAL SHARDS, THE STOLEN Whiptail slowly came into view.

"That's it," whispered Neil. "Now . . . what exactly do we do?" The radio was still out, and Neil didn't quite feel like asking Boris for help.

"The electromagnetic pulse cannon," said JP.

"It's what Dallas trained us on," said Waffles, punching his brother in the shoulder, excited at the mere chance of making something explode.

"From level five in Shuttle Fury. Remember?" added

JP. "It would prevent the *Newt* from escaping, and we could safely tow the craft home."

Neil had never heard of such a thing, but his crew didn't have to know that, necessarily. He was slowly picking up some of the tricks of the trade for being in charge. Things like not telling the complete truth seemed to be cheat codes in the world of bossing people around.

"Pulse cannon, right. Duh," Neil said. "Dale, prepare the pulse cannon. We've got to recover that ship."

But before any type of target lock could be made on the stolen Whiptail, the *Newt* turned to face Neil and his band of astronauts.

"Careful, they could be trying to pulse cannon us! Who knows who's in there," said Sam. "Or what that ship does."

Neil knew she was correct, and he banked the *Fossil* right, engaging the thrusters on the left side of the ship. Even in a dangerous situation, he loved the feeling of piloting in space. Instead of his power only coming from the four glowing jets at the rear of the craft, he was able to maneuver his ship with propulsion from all sides. Possibilities were endless.

As the ship slid through the black sky, Neil squinted

to look into the cockpit of the ship opposite him. He spotted a silhouette.

Two silhouettes, actually. And they seemed . . . *small*. Maybe even smaller than Neil, which was saying something.

Are they just kids?

With a quick spin, the stolen ship suddenly shot off, a billion-dollar speck of technology whizzing next to Earth.

"Not so fast!" Neil yelled as he propelled the spacecraft after them. Without gravity to contend with, the ship responded to even the tiniest of turns and corrections.

Any real pilot would've already pulled a move on me. These people are amateurs.

Neil felt the adrenaline of an entire night of gaming begin to rush through his body. The mission was about to be a success, and in record time for Commander Finch. Neil would be back soon to recount the story to the commander, and probably to Jones, too. They'd be three veteran pilots talking feats of bravery.

But you're not done yet.

As he drew close enough to get a visual on the stolen craft, its white-and-black sides stamped with the NASA logo, it escaped into some kind of hyperdrive. It looked like a blue orb burst out from the rocket engine, which sent the Whiptail screeching deep into the starry galaxy.

"Warp speed! Warp speed!" the other gamers shouted at Neil.

"Yes! That's what I'm saying!" Neil said, hoping someone would kick the hyperdrive into gear on their ship. But the ship kept on at its regular velocity as the stolen craft completely disappeared from the radar. The beeping detection system went silent.

"Neil," Trevor said slowly, his voice eerily calm. It reminded Neil of a scary movie, the kind where an evil boy shows up in your basement every night. "Why didn't you pull the warp-speed lever?"

Neil's face turned a deep amber, and his voice began to get tense in embarrassment.

"I, uh . . . ," Neil stammered sheepishly as he fumbled with the controls. He didn't even know there *was* a warp-speed lever.

"Yeah, Neil. What gives?" JP added.

Much like his attempts at it before, Neil's foray into lying caught up to him—and this time the fate of his crew and the mission was in the balance.

"Take a chill pill, everyone. Neil has gotten us this far. He might have just had a brain malfunction. I get those all the time when I eat organic Cheetos," Biggs said.

"Neil?" Sam asked. She could see that Neil was far from his normal color. "Is Trevor right . . . ?"

Neil decided that there was no better moment for the truth.

"Um, well. Full disclosure: I didn't know there was a warp speed," he admitted. "I never really finished that game . . . and I hid a couple packets of space ice cream in my jumpsuit."

His fellow gamers went silent, their disappointment leeching into the air. Neil could almost feel their anger weighing him down.

"'Tisn't true, is it, Master Andertol?" asked Riley, his voice dripping with Olde English disbelief.

"You're no commander," scowled Trevor.

The remaining groans all washed together, deflating Neil even further. But the next voice he heard was the one that hurt the most. The voice that had been with him for all-night gaming sessions and rescuing top secret military intel, both as a boy and a girl.

"You mean you didn't finish the game? Or you

didn't play it?" asked Sam. "Because what about all those times I asked to practice with you? And you said you'd just finished?"

Neil knew he was sticking to the truth from then on.

"Basically, I played the game for probably an *hrfhr*," Neil said.

"I'm sorry, say that again?" said Trevor.

"For an hour."

"An hour a day?" asked Harris.

"Like an hour total? And there's a good chance there was a bathroom break for thirty-five of those minutes," Neil confessed.

"Really, dude?" asked Biggs. He looked at Neil with disgust as everyone leaned in their seats to face Neil. "Oh. That's why you said that lame joke twice. You were just trying to butter up Finch."

Trevor angrily unhooked himself from his tiny chimp seat and drifted over to Neil. He tore the commander pin from Neil's chest, and then he pinned it to his own.

"Only real commanders get to wear this," Trevor sneered as he grasped Neil's controls. "You've lost your piloting privilege."

"And to make sure you don't get any ideas, how about this?" Neil's still-real-life nemesis said as he peeled a freeze-dried banana and smushed it down over Neil's pilot joystick. "No touching. And tell you what, you should just go down to the middeck. With Boris."

Neil felt like a complete failure. He not only proved Jones was wrong, but he let down his friends. Plus, he was worried about going to the deck below—that chimpanzee looked like a biter.

Neil began to unfasten himself from his commander's chair. As the twelve pseudo-astronauts looked out into the emptiness of space, they all couldn't help but feel scared and alone.

CHAPTER 17

"COMMANDER TREVOR HAS DECLARED THAT YOU SHALL remain with the crew, but serving at the lowest possible rank," said Biggs as he escorted Neil from his chair in the front, following an order from the person now in charge.

"Cabin boy," Trevor said. "And it's Captain Trevor. Actually, Space-Pirate Captain Trevor Grunsten."

"Are you kidding?" Neil replied.

"Every great pirate captain always needed a good cabin boy," Trevor reassured.

"Have you been watching too much History

Channel?" Neil said. "Pirates? Cabin boys? This is ridiculous."

"Silence, cabin boy! Down with Boris you go!" Trevor barked, craning his neck toward Neil. "We've got to complete our mission and get back to Finch."

"I'm not going down with that mean monkey. Did you see that scar on his face? I feel like he's seriously maimed a zookeeper, if not worse," Neil said defiantly.

"Go downstairs. Or else," said Trevor. His voice had a relaxed evilness to it, and it made Neil actually feel uncomfortable. Trevor turned back to JP. "I wish we still lived in a world where swordplay was encouraged."

"But it is! In the magical land of the Faire!" Riley exclaimed. "You must come for a visit, and you can joust with Sir Keith the Brave! Or just eat roast turkey legs, carefully prepared by Sir Randy the Line Cook!"

Trevor's face crinkled in disgust as he took firm hold of the ship's controls.

Neil tried to float away angrily, but he wasn't exactly sure how to go about doing so. He ended up looking like a wobbling ballerina before he reached the rear of the ship's cabin. He looked down to see the hatch leading downstairs to the ship's middeck and hesitated while grabbing the handle. It was like the boiler room of the ship, and Boris's quarters. Neil's watch read 17:45. It was still Saturday evening.

"Well, we can at least get out of this space junk so nothing hits us," the new commander said. "I never realized how much crud was just flying around out here."

Trevor placed his hands on the ship's exterior thruster controls and steered clear of immediate danger, but he seemed hesitant to floor it. Their Whiptail could do things previously thought impossible, but right now it was simply puttering through the vacuum of the universe.

"We need a shield or armor or something," Trevor said, "while we try to figure out wherever the heck that ship just went."

"Lord Trevor, if it is a shield you need, I can fashion one for you," said Riley. "Just find for me a turtle shell, and as many leather pieces as you can spare."

"Where are you from? Can we send you back?" Trevor hissed at Riley. "JP, I'm not sure if this chimpanzee ship is made for rough use. We need to get out of this debris. And, cabin boy, I said downstairs!"

Neil had been lingering at the door leading to the

middeck, not ready to join a surly Russian chimpanzee. But as he pulled open the floor's hatch, rhythmic beeps bounced through the shuttle's cockpit. It was the radar, coming back to life as the crew sat in uncertain silence.

"Well, what are we waiting for?" shouted Waffles. "We've found our stolen ship, so follow that beeping! Chop-chop!"

But now-Commander Trevor hesitated. He wriggled in his seat, and the short strands of his hair stood on end and waved like tall grass.

"Without any contact with our CAPCOM, or anyone really, I think it's best to head back to base," Sam said. "What else didn't Finch tell us? Doesn't this whole mission seem ridiculous to anyone else? Is the sun about to explode, too?"

"Well, if that's the case, we need to stick around," said Biggs. "My grandma told me the sun was made of smiles and gumdrops. That thing's gonna burst like a piñata full of happiness."

"No, seriously!" Sam said, her voice impatient. "What if they can't reach us to say we don't have enough oxygen? Or worse?"

Neil's eyes narrowed. She had a very real point.

"Sam's right," Neil said. "Something's feeling unusual."

"Oh, unusual, you say? And now we'll take orders from the *cabin boy*?" Trevor said, making a weird snorting noise.

"Again, that's not even a real position!" Neil said, but he could sense arguing was worthless.

"JP, get me the coordinates of that bogey. This mission's only just begun," Trevor ordered.

"This is what you get when you put boys in charge," Sam grumbled.

Controlling gas puffs from the ship's exterior control jets, Trevor steered the shuttle away from the giant rolling sphere of Earth. Neil grabbed tightly to Waffles's seat.

As Trevor steered the ship, the moon slowly entered into view in the cockpit's window, half-covered in shadows. The beeping of the radar grew louder, signaling that the stolen ship was somewhere near the orbiting chunk of space rock.

"Anyone getting a visual on the *Newt*?" asked Trevor, easing on the ship's jets.

The nose of the ship coasted toward the moon.

Neil could see huge craters dotting its surface. Some

were tiny, but others looked the size of shopping malls.

"Our target's location is just into the far side of the moon . . . ," JP said, his eyes scanning the sleek screens ahead of him. "The hemisphere that's always covered in shadows."

"And is it safe to venture into these shadows?" asked Riley.

"We'll see. It looks like the Whiptail has landed on the moon," JP answered.

Trevor guided the shuttle toward the moon's surface, its shadow cast over unending craters. It stopped just before entering darkness.

With barely any sun, Neil saw just how endlessly dark the universe was. This whole outer-space thing was beginning to feel like being stuck in a pitch-black forest without a flashlight or gaming device. There seemed to be way fewer s'mores in the cosmos, though.

"*Booooop*," hummed the radar. The manic beeps were now a constant tone. Whatever they were after was right below them.

"Beginning landing maneuvers," announced Trevor, who skillfully propelled the shuttle downward. The ship's landing gears unfolded and made contact with the surface as exterior jets sprayed dust and rocks in all directions.

"Um, not seeing a ship, boss," said Dale, nearly stretching out of his seat to get a better view. He was right. Whatever was giving the radar fits was supposedly dead ahead, but twelve sets of eyes only saw craggy landscape.

"We should get out and search," said Harris. "Could be behind us, or in one of these craters. They're probably trying to hide again."

"I was just going to suggest that," said Trevor, most likely lying. "We'll cover more ground if we fan out."

Should we really leave our ship?

Neil's impulse was to say something, but he thought better of it. Trevor would probably lock him in a cabin boy cell while the crew went exploring, so he was the first to open the rear door leading to the yellow air lock.

The crew bounced out of their seats, smashing against computers lining the cramped ship's walls. They weren't totally weightless, but Neil felt like he weighed as much as a bowling ball. One of those really light ones you could chuck overhanded.

"Everybody suit up," said Trevor, who was crawling

into one of the white space suits attached to the walls of the air lock. "Cabin boys last."

Neil rolled his eyes and looked at the space-walking outfits. They were in two pieces, connected with a sturdy metal ring at the center. Each suit had a white backpack full of oxygen and various other life-supporting instruments.

"Ow!" yelled Corinne as Riley jabbed her eye with his glove. The close quarters made for a very interactive costume change.

Securing his suit with two clicks, Neil changed. Even Harris had his suit on, and he was checking his oxygen levels on a small monitor on the left sleeve. Neil did the same, and Waffles pulled open the door leading to cabin.

"We're leaving for a little bit, but we'll be back, Boris!" yelled Dale through his helmet, as if he were leaving a dog at home on a school day. A chimpanzee shriek carried into the air lock, but everybody agreed it sounded like the good kind of ape yell. The twin brothers pulled the cabin door shut tightly.

"Okay, everybody, everyone have three green lights on their suit monitor?" asked Sam, making sure each suit was working perfectly. The group confirmed as Neil looked at the bulky suit covering his left forearm.

"I do. How do you guys know all this stuff?" Neil said.

"It's in Shuttle Fury," she replied. "It's amazing what you can learn when you do the work you're supposed to do."

With that, Sam carefully opened the shuttle's side exit door. One by one they stepped outside. Neil was last, and he hopped out with a smile. His big white boots landed, leaving a pair of size-nine footprints.

CHAPTER 18

IN ALMOST PITCH-DARKNESS, THE GROUP FANNED OUT, leaping in huge strides as if they were dangling from bungee cords. Everyone clicked on the flashlights built into their rectangular backpacks.

"Race to that thing!" shouted Waffles, pointing to a huge triangular rock that slimmed down to a rounded point.

Neil did his best to sprint in a suit that felt like over-size hockey gear, and he leaped with both legs forward. "Ow," Neil said as his feet hit something and knocked him on his back. He righted himself, like a lunar turtle.

It felt like he'd kicked a boulder, but when he looked down, he couldn't see anything besides small moon rocks. He put his arm forward, and it made contact, too. Neil flattened his palms and pushed against the invisible force. It was like a wall that curved upward, and Neil couldn't tell where it ended.

"Hey . . . guys?"

Neil pushed forward, hard. Whatever it was didn't budge, and it continued well beyond what Neil could reach.

"You know something? This feels like . . . ," Neil murmured.

"What?" Harris asked, bounding over to Neil.

"Like that bubble you made with the Chameleon scales from your island. But this is different. You can't pass through this. "

Harris reached out a hand and felt as well, nodding in agreement.

"Yeah. It must be an actual structure," Harris said. "I was just broadcasting a projection."

They kept their hands on the object's side and walked in separate directions, covering more ground to feel for the edge of the building.

"Wait, got something here!" Neil yelled. He patted his hands ahead of him, and he could feel the outline of something.

"It's a door!"

Neil found and grasped its handle as Harris waddled over, followed by Sam and Biggs.

Okay, there's probably not some type of bear waiting for me on the other side of this door, right?

"So what are you gonna do?" asked Biggs, his curly hair a mess inside his helmet.

"What do you think he's gonna do? He's gonna open it, Granola Gary," said Harris. Neil laughed, but he felt a little bad.

He tugged at the oblong handle, and a door opened up to a completely visible air lock similar to the one in their spaceship. The outside of the door and struc-ture were, in fact, cloaked by some kind of invisibility technology.

"Hey, dudes! We've got a door situation over here. Come check it out!" Biggs radioed to his fellow astro-nauts. He waved the rest of his team in, and they piled inside the cramped air lock that sort of felt like a janitor's closet. Jason 2 was the last inside and pulled the outer door shut, twisting a giant metal door handle. The interior was lit by small LED bulbs.

"So what do we do once we open this?" Sam asked.

"Well, if this is an alien, I want everyone to know they can't read your mind if you're thinking about volcanoes," said Biggs. "I've been doing some research."

"Seriously, though. I bet whoever stole the ship is hiding out in here," Sam said. "What's our plan?"

"Did we have a plan last time? I say we just tackle anything we see," said Waffles, getting a little jacked up.

Neil nodded, and he and Sam both pushed the heavy interior door open.

Each astronaut twisted into a defensive stance, ready for whatever was lurking beyond a rusty-looking door. But as Neil and Sam pushed it wide open, they were greeted by quite the opposite—what could only be described as a lush space paradise. The door was near a patch of stubby palm trees, but just beyond them was beautifully green grass.

In the exact center was a vibrant garden with exotic flowers and vegetables somehow thriving. It was surrounded by maybe twenty buildings in total, equally spaced in a circle within the biodome. It looked like a village. All the structures were off-white and dome shaped, looking like two-story yurts Neil had seen in a Canadian wilderness documentary.

"Good find, cabin boy," said Trevor, plucking a ripe green pepper from a stalk.

"Yeah, nicely done, *Neil*," said Biggs. It was relieving to hear at least somebody actually call him by a real name.

The secret building was a dome made of thick glass, kind of like a cosmic greenhouse. The atmosphere inside seemed very alive and welcoming, especially compared to the desolation outside.

"While I can't be certain, it does appear that the environment inside this bubble can sustain human life," said JP. "We might be able to take off these helmets to conserve our oxygen."

Neil felt weird at the mere thought of detaching the helmet sustaining his existence, like removing a life jacket in the middle of the ocean.

What if this glass dome has a leak in it? Is it safe to take this thing off?

"Space corn!" said Riley, his helmet already off as he ripped an ear of corn from a sturdy stalk.

"Riley, you have to boil—" Biggs warned, but it was too late. Riley chomped into the pale uncooked kernels, his teeth barely sinking in.

"Sweet Odysseus!" he yelped, tenderly clutching his mouth.

"Well, at least we know it's safe to take off these helmets," Jason 1 said. "Thanks for being the guinea pig on that one."

"Nary a problem."

After watching Riley and Jason 1 continue to breathe normally, Neil unhooked his helmet from his space suit. It made a sound like opening a soda can, followed by a heavy click. Neil took a deep breath of the filtered biodome air. It was safe and crisp, and it smelled like freshly cut grass. He jumped up and down a few times, enjoying the reduced gravity found on the moon's surface.

"What's a nudist colony?" asked Corinne.

"What? Is that what this place is?" Neil said, shocked. "Then we've gotta get out of here. Stat."

"No," Corinne corrected. "The New Dist. It's printed all over everything in here." Neil looked at a watering can near a patch of space tomatoes, and he saw the block lettering with the same title stamped onto the side.

"No clue, must be whatever this place is," Neil said. He walked up to a door marked POD 12. He raised his hand to knock, but stopped after hearing something just on the other side.

Why was this showing up on our radar? Is this where our stolen Whiptail is?

"What are you waiting for, an invitation?" said Trevor as he barged in front of Neil, flinging the door open.

But inside the building wasn't an elaborate scientist's workshop, or a top secret laser telescope. Inside looked like a regular house, with simply a couch, a television, and a pale boy in red sweatpants. Sprawled out on the sofa, he was playing a game on a high-definition TV.

As the choppy graphics and bright stars whizzed by, it was unmistakably the one game that would now haunt Neil's dreams forever—Shuttle Fury.

CHAPTER

19

★ ★ ★

BEWILDERED AND DELIGHTED, THE BOY JUMPED UP. JASON 1 and Jason 2 both pushed back-to-back, joining their arms in a defensive martial art combo stance. But the boy was friendly and simply smiled, throwing his controller on the couch after exiting his game.

"Whoa! Visitors!" he said, brushing pieces of caramel corn from his sweatpants.

"Are you an alien?" Biggs demanded. "Because I'm thinking of the biggest volcano ever."

The boy laughed, which helped put Neil more at ease.

"I'm Lars," he introduced, waving a bony hand.

He had comically large ears and a curving nose that wheezed with each breath.

"I can assure you guys I'm not an alien," the boy said, which was probably exactly what an alien would say. "I'm from Nova Scotia. Just a scientist's kid trapped up here in a space bubble."

"What is this place?" asked Sam. "This isn't an international lab, and something tells me this isn't available public info."

"Indeed, not really," Lars said. "It's basically a self-sustaining community. It was built in secret a couple years ago by a group of countries and private space companies, to test if humans could survive away from Earth."

And steal top secret space shuttles? Neil was still a bit skeptical of this stranger.

"The New District Colony," he said, with a proud smile.

"Is that like one of those groups where everyone has to wear cloaks and identical white sneakers?" asked Biggs.

"No, it's just a cool name," Lars explained. "Or I guess it is. All the adults here named it and stamped it all over the place."

- -

"Cool. I'm Biggs, it's nice to meet you."

The two shook hands, and Biggs made a sign with both hands, like he was holding a fishing rod that was on fire. Lars looked puzzled and turned to Neil for an explanation.

"Oh, he's been creating his own sign language," Neil explained. "I think that means it's good to meet you?"

"It means 'Thanks for the hospitality, moon child.' But close," said Biggs. "Also, might I suggest a new abbreviation for this whole colony? You're gonna attract a lot of space riffraff. Unless that's the type of thing you're going for."

Lars nodded his head slightly, as if that wasn't the first time he'd heard the suggestion.

"So what do you guys like doing? Puzzles? I've got some of those around here somewhere," he said. He seemed frantic. "Video games? I have lots of those."

"You may just be talking to the twelve best video gamers alive," Neil said. "Well, our friend Yuri is at home puking. So just know there could be thirteen of the best living gamers here."

"Oh, you don't say?" Lars said as he reached into a

slim freezer and pulled out a bag of dehydrated French fries. He emptied its contents into a machine that looked like a platinum-blue microwave and sounded like a tiny leaf blower. He punched a few buttons and began pulling cups from the cupboard above.

Lars held up the glasses to the track lighting overhead, squinting to determine if they were clean before lining them up. He wiped some stray cheese balls from his counter with his forearm.

"Check it out, ultimate cheese ball toss," Lars said, flipping a yellow fake-cheese puff in the air. It floated in a gentle arc, barely creeping through the air as it rotated. With a spring from his feet, Lars bounced up to bite the neon snack from the air. Neil wondered what kind of distance he could get tossing a doughnut hole.

Lars seemed not to eat in front of others very often. He took huge bites of caramel corn with an open mouth and wiped the mess from the corners of his mouth onto his shirtsleeve. His shirt was a gray skintight turtleneck that had THE NEW DIST COLONY plastered to it in black lettering.

Neil knew he was getting a lucky glimpse into the lifestyle constant video gaming without parental supervision provided. He wondered how one might go about getting accepted into the New Dist Colony.

As Lars scrambled in the kitchen's cupboards, Sam and the rest of the group had begun slyly snooping around Lars's house. After all, the radar for the missing ship did lead them here. Something was going on with this bubble boy.

They poked through a counter of snacks and riffled through a small stack of video games near the entertainment system.

"You guys should see downstairs," Lars said, his arms full of snacks for the crew. "I've got low-gravity Ping-Pong, and I just got a new space dartboard. There's an even bigger TV and a stock of space junk food. We can see who wants to play me in my favorite game."

"Shuttle Fury?" asked Neil, shakily clutching a tray holding twelve cups of a purplish space juice poured by Lars.

"Wow, yeah! I didn't think anybody else played it."

"I don't, really," Neil admitted.

"Oh, Lars, our friend Neil here *loves* to play that game," said Sam, her voice caked with sarcasm. Neil clenched his teeth and gave his friend a glare, but she only responded with a pleasant smile.

Does nobody even care anymore that Finch put me in charge?

"We can all go downstairs, and you two can play a nice long game up here. Sound good, Neil?" said Sam. He knew she was probably buying time for them to figure out what was going on with the radar, but Neil didn't enjoy being kept upstairs with their bizarre new friend.

"Awesome," Lars said, pointing to a silver door in the corner of the room. "You guys go make yourselves at home downstairs. We can play all night! And on the moon it's sort of always night, so we can just play forever!"

Only a fraction of his normal weight, Waffles was the first to run toward the basement door, slamming into it.

"Still gettin' the hang of jumping," Waffles said as he rubbed his forehead. The others followed him as he opened the door to the basement, flipping on the light switch.

"You've got to do more of a skipping motion, like an injured pony," Lars explained, hopping toward the small dirty kitchen. "You'll get used to it."

Neil stayed put as he watched his friends moon-leap toward the basement. Harris and Sam walked together, and Harris said something only Sam could hear. Neil could see her giggle, and some kind of emotion caused Neil's stomach to drop.

CHAPTER

20

"WHERE ARE THE ADULTS?" NEIL SAID, SLURPING ON A PUR-plish space beverage. Looking around the messy space bubble, Neil had the impression an adult hadn't been present for months. "And who are these adults? My mom would lose it if my room looked like this. Well done."

Neil walked over and plopped down on the chair, an action that took a bit longer than it usually did on Earth. Each time he easily lifted off the ground, Neil felt like a wrestler leaping off a top rope for a high-flying elbow drop.

"My pleasure," Lars said with a laugh, his voice nasal and slow. "The adults are all scientists. I'm the only one here under the age of fifty."

"Where are they now?"

"A long weekend trip to the other side of the moon. Another country sent a rover up here to explore, so they're off to go mess with it," Lars said. He started Shuttle Fury, selecting a head-to-head battle round. "They have big Sasquatch costumes and everything. Scientists on vacation are weird."

You're telling me.

Neil's father was a scientist as well, although his specialty was archaeology and things that happened millions of years ago. He also was horrible on vacations, constantly keeping to a strict schedule and dressing in all tan like a sunburned zookeeper.

"You ready?" said Lars, his green eyes opened wide. Neil responded with a nod, and the game erupted with lights and sounds of space shuttles. The level featured a race to random coordinates about halfway from the moon and Mars. Lars jumped out to an early start, but Neil was able to keep pace.

As they played the game, successfully rolling their

ships through an asteroid belt, Neil soon realized Lars was good—like, really good. He rarely encountered players that could flat-out outplay him. Lars would soon notch his tenth victory in a row.

"Wow, Lars. You're really great."

Maybe Lars was just a totally normal guy, simply stuck here with his dad.

"Yeah, I've had a lot of time to just practice," Lars said, before tapping a series of buttons on his controller. His shuttle discarded extra weight from the payload air lock underneath, increasing the shuttle's speed.

"Whoa, cool!" Neil said.

"And do you know the trick to warp speed?"

I don't think I'll ever forget it. Nobody is going to let that go.

"Yeah, I think," Neil said as he activated the warp speed shown to him by his friends. His ship barreled ahead of Lars's, leaving a glittering blue trail of space dust in its wake.

"Oh, that's just regular warp speed," Lars said, a bit unimpressed. "But this is even cooler."

Flipping a couple buttons on the control panel, Lars throttled forward. His ship jumped into what looked like a double-warp drive, going even faster than the trick Trevor annoyingly demonstrated before.

Lars's craft shot into the distance, slowly corkscrewing as it left an even broader blue trail behind it.

"Man, I played this game for hours and never even saw this!" Neil exclaimed. "Or, at least, I know people who have played this game for hours, and they've never seen this!"

"Oh yeah. Some Whiptails don't have it, but you can use all your reserve fuel to kinda do the same thing," Lars said, snorting. "You can't unlock this until the last level. That and the Whiptail's last line of defense. Supposedly it's how you destroy the asteroid in the game, when you're out of pulse cannon energy and you've discharged your missiles."

Wait, asteroid?

"I've tried it, but my ship always explodes," Lars said. "There's some trick with it I'm not seeing. I'll figure it out. Like I said, I have a lot of time up here."

"I'd imagine," said Neil, his tongue curling out of the corner of his mouth. His mouth stretched into a smile as he successfully pulled off the same double-warp maneuver.

"Although things have gotten a bit better lately."

"Oh yeah?"

"Totally. I learned a new trick on the Whiptail shuttle. You can jump-start it from outside of the ship," Lars said as he landed his virtual spaceship.

"Oh, without it moving first? That could've been helpful," said Neil.

Lars looked at him with a quizzical face but kept playing the shuttle simulator. His character, a boxy pilot, took robotic steps out of the air lock. The avatar shut the round door and slid a secret panel that was just above the doorway. Inside was a red handle. It kind of looked like a fire alarm.

"Cool," said Neil, wondering if his ship outside had the same feature. Lars's character tugged on it and ran backward, watching the rockets on the back of the simulated Whiptail begin to bloom white and blue.

"I'm excited you guys are here. We can get a big team game when those twins come back, too," Lars said. "They promised to come back soon."

Hold it, Neil thought.

"Twins?"

"Yeah, they stopped by within the last twelve hours

or so," Lars replied, now almost a light-year ahead of Neil in the virtual race. "You need to ease off on all the throttling. Flying in space is different."

Lars fired a laser at floating space rocks, leaving jagged obstacles for Neil to encounter.

"Were they alone?" Neil asked.

"You sure ask a lot of questions. Yeah, they came by themselves," Lars said. "They knew all the tricks to this game, which was impressive. I actually came close to losing a game. I tried to make them hang out longer, but they were in a rush. Something about . . ."

"What?"

"Why are you so interested in this?" asked Lars, looking away from the screen.

"I'm just a curious guy."

"Well, curious guy, they were looking for their parents, or something."

Neil's eyebrows lifted with this new information, and his ship began to float idly.

It all made sense. The Minor twins stole the rocket because they wanted to look for their long-lost parents.

They're the ones I saw in the window of the stolen ship.

It was definitely time to go. Neil purposefully steered

his ship into the path of a behemoth meteoroid, and the craft was quickly smashed apart like a golf cart stuck on railroad tracks.

"Game over. Darn," Neil said. "Guys!"

Neil ran downstairs.

"We have to go. I think I know where to look for the missing spaceship!"

"Not so fast," Lars said, appearing at the basement door. He had a mischievous smile, and he clicked a button on a small handheld remote he had kept in his sweatpants. They heard the sound of a heavy metal bolt locking the front door in place.

"You're not going anywhere."

CHAPTER 21

"YOU CAN'T LEAVE," LARS SHOUTED, HIS VOICE HEATED. "I'M sick of being up here all alone."

Neil imagined it could get pretty lonely planted on the moon all alone. It seemed a lot like being stranded in a field in the middle of nowhere, like a cowboy.

Space cowboys. Oh, now I get it.

"If you think there's any chance we're staying in here, you're sorely mistaken," yelled Trevor, trying to stomp angrily toward Lars. In the low gravity, however, it was still a gentle bouncing, and not at all what he was going for. "My dad doesn't practice space law, but I'm sure he could start."

"You think anybody knows what goes on up here? Ha!" Lars said, which made Neil feel nervous. In space nobody could hear you yell for help against a turtle-necked tween, and that went double inside a glass dome. "I've known you were after those kids the whole time. Do you think I'm stupid?"

"I get that it must be lonely up here, but we need to go," Neil said. Trevor and Waffles tugged at the door's metal handle, but it refused to budge.

"We've got some serious stuff to attend to."

Lars's face was covered in shadows, and his features that seemed goofy and friendly before now appeared sinister. His head tilted slightly forward, and the circles under his eyes grew shades darker.

"Serious stuff?" Lars questioned. "Stuff pertaining to how, exactly, twelve kids just showed up at my invisible moon habitat?"

"Well, what about you? Why is your little space condo showing up on our radar?" said JP.

"New Dists welcome everyone. We have a constant radar beacon welcoming any intelligent life-form," Lars said. "But I'm beginning to wonder more about you all. Especially where you found these very realistic NASA outfits."

Neil hesitated, unsure what to admit. Even if he hinted at the truth, where would he begin explaining the situation?

You see, we're a group of gamers working for the US military. We did one tour a few months back, and now we've flown to space with little training in a spaceship full of space bananas as Earth's last hope. It was all completely understandable.

Neil heard clanging at the door, and turned to see Waffles and Dale attempting to wedge dinner knives into every possible crevice.

"You can mess with that door as much as you like, but every exit is sealed shut with reinforced steel," Lars said with a snarl. "The New District just doubled its population."

★ ★ ★

Neil's watch beeped, reading 03:00. It was closing in on a full twenty-four hours since they'd left NASA, and the *Newt* was probably long gone, its warp drive kicking up stardust throughout the galaxy. Neil and the others took naps, waking up in shifts to do battle with Lars.

"Forty-seven straight victories!" blared Lars's froggy voice.

What initially seemed like a fortress of never-ending joy and gaming was now a prison. A prison with video games, yes, but a prison nonetheless.

Thus far Lars had gone undefeated on head-to-head matchups in space Ping-Pong, space foosball, and Shuttle Fury, possibly proving he should've been selected to pilot the secret mission in the first place.

"Who's up next? I'm beginning to think we may not have any more challengers," Lars said with an arrogant tone. He seemed to lack awareness about the benefits of sharing and playing nice with others. And hygiene, for that matter. But he was a ruthless pilot.

"You'd think he'd get sick of beating everyone repeatedly on that stupid game," Harris said to Neil as the two sat down on Lars's couch on the main floor. After an hour of silently snooping around every exit for a point of weakness, they'd given up hope of an escape. Lars's lunar home was on lockdown.

"Looks like we'll just have to plan to grow old in this place," Jason 2 said, joining the couch with a joke.

Nobody laughed, but Neil could tell Harris's brain was busy thinking through something.

"Hey, Harris, you're next," said Lars from the bottom of the basement staircase.

"Dude, you already beat me once," Harris yelled back. "I get it; you're very good at games involving the space program. Call me when you play a game with some real action."

Neil could hear scuffling from the floor below, followed by Lars reappearing at the top of the stairway.

"What's that supposed to mean?" Lars said, looking offended. "Shuttle Fury is hands down the—"

"Save it, Moonboy," Harris said, unapologetic for cutting him off. Neil could see flashes of the attitude that made him a formidable villain. He could really get under your skin. "You want to have a video game challenge, let's up the stakes."

Lars looked shocked and intrigued. His boogery-nose breath subtly whistled in the recycled space air.

"We play one game of my choice," Harris explained. "I win, you let us out of this little space shack. You win, we take you to an actual spaceship, like the ones you pilot in the game. The real deal."

"What's the game?" said Lars, looking unimpressed by news of a ship. JP, Riley, and the others filtered into the room, watching as Harris gave away their prized possession.

"The highly anticipated sequel to Feather Duster, *Bird and Beast Magazine*'s number three ostrich-themed virtual reality," Harris said.

"What?"

"Feather Duster 2," Harris said as he reached into a pocket of his suit and brandished a clear case housing a silver disc. With it were two masks that looked a lot like ostrich beaks. "Complete with smells."

Lars said nothing and stood in silence, possibly calculating his odds at victory.

"If I win, each one of you has to play an hour of games with me a day," Lars added. "I'll sleep twelve hours and play twelve hours."

"When will you eat?" asked Corinne.

"We'll cross that bridge when we get there," Lars said. "And another thing: I'm not playing you. I'm playing *him*."

Lars pointed a clammy finger directly at Neil.

"If he's as good at this Feather Duster game as he is at Shuttle Fury, this will be a piece of cake."

"Deal," said Harris, not giving Neil a chance to respond.

Neil shot him a look, remembering how when Neil was Harris's prisoner, Neil played him for his release. It ended with Neil being returned as a prisoner, despite being victorious. Plus he hadn't had a chance to play the newest version of the long-awaited sequel.

"Why should Neil get to play? I want to challenge this worm," said Trevor, attempting to remind everyone he was still in charge.

"No. No, it's perfect," Harris said, trying to hide a smile. "Neil and Lars. *Feather Duster 2: Eclectic Bugaboo, Smells Edition version three-point-oh.*"

Harris tossed the game disc to Biggs, who slipped it into the console connected to the TV. He punched on the power to both, and the screen lit up with a flapping ostrich, with much more detail than the first game Harris had created.

"Wow, this new screen looks great," said Neil as he grabbed one of the two controllers sprawled on the small coffee table. His joystick controlled a moving bag of ostrich pellets. They looked just like the ones Neil fed

Regina. He tapped a button and fed a few to the strutting ostrich wandering around the starting menu.

"And you guys are gonna love the smell technology," said Biggs, securing an ostrich beak to each competitor. Neil wasn't surprised to see Harris carrying these around in his backpack. "I think we've really worked out some of the kinks this time around."

It would be exciting to see what Biggs and Harris had worked on. Neil wondered if Biggs's made-up sign language would appear in the next installment.

"So the match will be two laps, standard bird specs. Lars, you choose the level," Harris explained.

Lars scrolled through the levels menu on the game and chose "Suburb Sprinter."

"Nice choice," Harris said. "Controls are the same as the first one, but you really just need sprint and jump. Eating potted plants gives you a speed boost, and watch out for neighbors with leaf blowers and sprinklers; they'll make you wipe out."

The two boys each controlled an ostrich, the screen divided in half. After a quick three-second countdown, the race began. The ostriches sped down an asphalt street, candy-colored houses lining the sides. The level looked like a neighborhood you could find anywhere, with curving pristine streets and cul-de-sacs full of crazed children.

Neil barely dodged a pigtailed girl riding a tricycle as his ostrich raced beyond one of the paved dead-end streets.

"Power up!" said an enthusiastic voice from the game as Neil's bird chomped down on a planted row of tulips. But Lars was a natural, and he kept pace with Neil. After biting through a patch of daisies, Lars even took the lead. Smells of freshly cut grass and hot charcoal grills oozed out from the fake beak.

Come on, Neil, you can't blow this.

"Final lap!" announced the game, after the two racing ostriches sprinted through the parking lot of a strip mall. But as they passed the open doors for smoothie joints and chain restaurants, the scents began to be a bit off.

Neil sniffled a few times, but instead of smelling bread outside of a bakery he was getting something else. It was more of a rotten-egg-meets-dirty-sock bouquet. He knew he couldn't let this distract him, and Neil forced himself not to think about the smells. He'd done it with the apple that got lost somewhere in his locker for all of seventh grade, so a minute longer was nothing.

"These smells are awful," Lars complained, catching a talon on a sprinkler. His ostrich fell a few steps behind Neil's. Basically everything was beginning to smell like a wet dog that lived in a pile of garbage.

"Sorry," Harris said. "We haven't beta tested some of these new scents." In Harris's eye, however, was a glint that made him seem anything but apologetic.

Lars tried smushing his nose against his shoulder to block his nostrils. There was only half a lap left, and his racing bird was actually neck and neck with Neil's. But suddenly his face turned an even ghostlier pale, and it looked like he could no longer take it. Lars dropped the controller to the ground and ripped off the smelly gadget wrapped around his face.

"Player two smell-forfeits!" declared the game. Lars's half of the screen turned a drab gray, while Neil's was soon filled with confetti.

"*Gaghhh,*" Lars gurgled as he punched a code into the keypad near the front door. "I need fresh garden oxygen!"

The door swung open, and Lars bolted out of sight.

"Quick, before it closes!" Harris yelled. Jason 1 Olympic-style long-jumped to wedge a foot in the doorway. The crew took off toward the New Dist Colony's exit.

"How did you know that would work?" Neil asked Harris as he and the others fastened their helmets back on. Harris smiled.

"We haven't been able to get the smells right. Pretty much everything Biggs has made recently smells like someone filled a watermelon with spoiled eggs. I knew they would start to get really gross," he explained.

"But I mean, how did you know I would last longer than Lars?" Neil asked. Harris laughed a few hard chuckles.

"Neil, no offense, but I've seen your room," Harris said. "That one video chat after your last mission? The amount of dirty laundry in there speaks for itself. That place was a swamp. I figured your smell tolerance was off the charts."

The group was giddy with the promise of freedom as they crammed into the tiny air lock once again. Everyone patted Harris on the back as they secured their helmets and space suits.

Sam shared a huge laugh with Harris, uncorking a bright smile Neil hadn't seen since a sun-kissed aircraft carrier somewhere in the Pacific Ocean.

Neil felt sheepish, especially at how hard Sam was laughing. It had more of a "laughing at you" feeling instead of a "laughing with you" he would have preferred.

Harris seemed to be getting the praise, but Neil was the one actually playing the game. But as they opened the air lock, leaving behind the New Dist Colony forever, Neil couldn't bounce away from the glass bubble fast enough.

CHAPTER 22

"GUYS. I KNOW WHERE WE SHOULD GO." SAID A CONFIDENT Harris, in the center of everyone huddled together in the *Fossil*'s air lock. They were waiting for a light with three green bananas, showing the air lock was pressurized and full of oxygen.

"I do, too, I think," Neil added. But the group was turned to Harris, apparently more anxious for his thoughts.

"Quiet, cabin boy, Pickles has an idea," said Trevor.

"The ISS. When I went up there before with my dad,

there were all sorts of scientists with crazy technology. They could find that ship in a second."

"I actually think we should—"

"Neil, you can play a game about ostriches, yes, but let the adults talk," said a sassy Waffles.

"You know what? Fine. I'm going down to middeck with Boris," said Neil, pushing through the crew as the air lock beeped. He unclicked the metal ring connecting his suit and squiggled out. "Apparently nobody wants to listen to me."

He opened the door to the ship's tiny main cabin and bounced over to the hatch on the floor, hitting his head on the ceiling. He lifted the hatch and effortlessly glided into the dimly lit room below. He could see Boris's eyes gleaming in the light of the equipment and wondered if he had just made a huge mistake.

★ ★ ★

"Boris, I'll be on this side, and you stay there. Everything will be cool," said Neil, his body pressed into a corner of the ship. The chimpanzee stood in his polyester suit and bared his teeth and gums at Neil before making a wet kissing motion. His lips were puckered, and Boris gave a quick shriek before going back to his task on the ship.

Neil tried to make out the gauges and levers Boris was constantly flicking and adjusting, but it seemed to make sense only to a primate. Everything had pictures of chimpanzees making hand signals. It really looked similar to Biggs's sign language, unbelievably.

Neil missed his friend Biggs. While he was just upstairs, this mission was different. Since Harris was pretty much Biggs's boss, Neil understood if things were a bit weird.

"Boris," said Neil, "maybe we can try communicating in other ways, instead of just screaming and throwing bananas at eyeballs." He was moving his hands around like he was churning butter. It was a rhythmic, calming motion Neil hoped might settle down his flight mate. He figured there was a 50 percent chance it was a sign for bacon.

Boris, however, replied by tossing a banana right at Neil. As they'd left the moon, the ship was once again in a zero-g environment, and the piece of yellow fruit cut a direct path to Neil's face.

"Ow," he said, rubbing his eye. Boris threw another, and a third. "What? What do you want, me to eat these?"

Boris smiled, chucking another bunch. Neil flung two back.

The food fight heated up, and Neil realized just how hungry he was. He grabbed a floating banana and started peeling it his normal way. It wasn't normal by most people's standards, but Neil always peeled it from the bottom up, splitting it on the peel seam. Boris grew excited and slapped the floor and ceiling with both hands.

"Oh, now you like me?" Neil mumbled through his banana. "At least there's somebody on this ship who does."

"*Pppbttt*," said Boris.

Boris peeled a banana just like Neil and took three delicate bites before peeling another.

Neil smiled, and he and Boris ate in silence. The chimp moved to sit next to Neil, and they relaxed between the bananas. Neil's head began bobbing, and eventually rested on the sturdy shoulder of the cosmonaut.

★ ★ ★

Neil could feel the ship slowing. They must be closing in on the ISS. He wedged his eyelids open. He and his chimpanzee friend had dozed off. Neil was surprised that the screaming primate from before was so good at cuddling. He wondered if one day he'd get to snuggle with Regina, if she didn't get too smelly . . . and if he ever made it home. His watch flashed 05:00.

Neil looked up through the machinery and banana peels. He couldn't allow himself to be stuck in the mid-deck all mission. If he'd learned anything from his food fight with Boris, it was that sometimes it helped to work out all the issues at once. He wanted to be part of the group again.

Untangling himself from the banana cargo nets, Neil floated up to the hatch. He pushed it open and crawled into the main cabin of the *Fossil*, followed by Boris.

"Hey, keep him downstairs; what if he freaks out and bites somebody?" yelled Trevor.

"I've been saying the same thing about you this whole trip," said Neil. "Boris is fine. He's the best friend I've got on this mission."

Neil noticed Harris had taken his seat in the front of the ship.

"Quiet, cabin boy," said Trevor. "I'm trying to command this mission."

"No. And I'm not a cabin boy. Finch made me commander," Neil said. "Listen, I know I messed up. But I can fix it."

"Really? Is there a black hole that would lead us to a dimension where you actually played Shuttle Fury?" said Sam.

"You're right; I shouldn't have lied about all that," admitted Neil. "But I can be there to help you guys. That's what a good commander does."

"Listen, Neil, you had a chance and you blew it. I'm sorry, but that's how life works," said Harris.

"Harris, no offense, but you wouldn't even be on here if not for me. You weren't invited," Neil said.

"Well, I think Neil should stay. We're a team, you guys," interrupted Biggs.

Neil took a deep breath. Biggs was right. He didn't want to fight with his friends; he just wanted to be included on the mission. "Thank you, my main man," he said to Biggs. "If no one objects, I'd like to stay on deck. If anyone has any objections, state them now."

Nobody spoke, and Neil settled himself into Yuri's seat. Boris jumped onto his lap and gave him a wet chimpanzee kiss. Sam turned around in her seat and gave him a smile, then she said, "No matter what Neil has done, he's still part of the group. We all mess up sometimes, but he didn't mean to hurt anyone."

Neil felt a warmth creep up his cheeks. Sam and Biggs had just really stood up for him.

Harris cleared his throat in embarrassment. "I feel obligated to say that I'm sorry, Neil. It's not something that I say often . . . but I wouldn't be here if it wasn't for you."

"Don't worry about it, Harris; we're glad to have you here."

And with that, it was basically like Neil had never almost entirely screwed up the mission. As they approached the ISS, Trevor slowed the ship to mimic the speed of the station. The International Space Station looked like a long fort with solar energy panels sticking off it.

"This is the *Fossil*, requesting permission to dock," said Biggs, manning the radio. "Do you copy, ISS?" Nobody replied. "This is an American shuttle looking for air-lock clearance. Do you copy, my dudes?"

There was no voice on the other end, and the crew watched the station float on.

"Should we try in Russian?" asked Sam. "Basically every astronaut has to be fluent."

"Yuri was the only one who could," said Jason 2. "Blast him and his weak stomach."

"I think it's just the radio in general. It hasn't seemed to be working since we crashed," said JP after investigating the issue further.

Neil stared down at Earth from nearly three hundred miles above. Had Neil known this would be how his weekend played out, he might have paid more attention to the planet he called home.

"Fine, we'll just let ourselves in," said Trevor. He guided the nose of the ship toward the orbiting station and spun the *Fossil*'s air-lock hatch to align with the ISS tunnel, forming an airtight seal.

"We are successfully docked," Trevor said smugly. "That's in level three if you were wondering, cabin boy Neil. Wanted you to see that one."

Waffles began to open the two doors of the *Fossil*'s air lock, now connected via tunnel to the ISS. The twelve astronauts fanned out to explore the station.

"Hello? Honey, we're home!" shouted Waffles. He looked left and right but saw only the empty interior of the giant laboratory. It was all white, with silver, black, and blue computers and screens bolted to every surface.

The station was eerily empty, and the electronics

seemed to be malfunctioning in waves, scrambling and surging off and then on again.

"The place is empty," said Jason 1, returning from a lap through the station.

"Guys," Sam said, sighing. "I vote we go back to Earth and get in touch with Finch. This is feeling weird."

Maybe she was right.

On a wall of electronics, Neil saw a radio. It had a small video screen.

"Do you think if you just press zero we can talk to an operator?" he said. JP looked at the equipment and tapped a few buttons. Soon everyone saw the image of Commander Finch. The screen was fuzzy, and lines of static kept washing over it.

"Recruits? He . . . *echs*—" Finch said, his words cutting in and out. Jason 1 slapped the screen.

"We're here, Commander Finch," said Sam, talking into a mic.

"You're coming in patchy," said Finch. "But I'll keep talking and hope this makes it to you."

He nervously swished his black mustache.

"I guess I saw something in all of you, and I let it cloud my judgment. I should never have sent you up there," Finch said. His voice was empty and defeated. "It was shortsighted and stupid."

Maybe Sam was right after all. Was something fishy happening with this mission?

"There's something you all need to know about Q-94," said the commander. "This mission is to . . ."

Uh-oh.

His transmission cut out.

From the far end of the station, a hatch opened. A woman appeared wearing a bright-red jumpsuit, the Chinese flag stitched to her left shoulder.

"Hey!" shouted Biggs.

She looked shocked, completely surprised to see twelve other people inside the ISS.

"What are you doing here?" she said, her pin-straight black hair drifting out as she floated toward them.

"Why is this place abandoned?" said Harris. "We need help finding a ship."

"There's no time for helping with anything," said the astronaut, her English choppy. "I'm getting in a Soyuz back to Earth for however long we have left. Do you need a ship? I can get you home, too, but we've got to go right now."

She was exasperated, beads of sweat collecting in the air around her.

"What do you mean, 'for however long we have left'?" asked Corinne.

"The asteroid."

"Yeah, we know," said Sam. "But that's like thirteen or so days away. We've got a mission to complete before then."

The astronaut looked startled.

"You don't understand. It was a miscalculation. Q-94. It is going to hit Earth in less than twenty-four hours."

CHAPTER

23

ASSURED THEY'D GET HOME ON THEIR OWN SHIP. THE ASTRO-
naut took off for her ride home.

Neil felt like he was in a closet of cotton balls.

*You mean Earth is going to be destroyed tomorrow? But
all my stuff is on Earth.*

"Neil, you there?" said Sam, snapping her fingers in
front of his face. "We're getting out of here. I think this
place is gonna go haywire or something from the magnetic field of the asteroid."

They drifted into the Whiptail, ready to take a last

ride home back to Earth. They huddled in the ship's air lock and waited for clearance from the automated system.

Neil looked at his watch, and it read 07:08. It was Sunday morning at home. Earth would be toast before homeroom Monday.

"Guys," said Neil.

No one paid attention.

"Guys," Neil tried again.

"Well, have we tried crafting some sort of asteroid hammock? Has this been discussed?" said Biggs.

"I think I know who stole the *Newt*."

Sam gave him a look.

"I think we're following the kids of Clint and Elle Minor," Neil said. "From what I heard from Lars, they're searching for their parents."

"Wait, those astronauts who disappeared like a year ago?" Sam asked.

"Exactly," Neil said. "Finch showed me their photo and talked about them having kids. I can't say for sure, but I just feel like it's no coincidence that two kids showed up at Lars's place, and we saw two tiny pilots flying that stolen Whiptail."

Silence filled the air lock again as the group let this new information sink in.

"Listen, I know I messed up before by not telling you guys I didn't play that game, but what have we got to lose?" Neil said to his crew. "I say we do what we can and try to find that ship. If we go back to Earth, it's the same as giving up."

"I propose a vote," said Riley. "For his courage and skill, we once again raise the name of young Andertol to commandant."

"Huh?" asked Jason 1.

"Commander Andertol is what he's saying," clarified Jason 2. "And I agree. Finch put Neil in charge; now we should, too. Who's in?"

Jason 2 raised his hand, followed by Sam, Harris, and Biggs.

"I can't raise a hand 'cause I think it's wedged in somebody's armpit, but I'm in," said Jason 1.

"Same," said Corinne and JP simultaneously.

"I'm with you, Neil. That's a majority of eleven votes," Dale said.

Trevor was the only person without a raised hand.

"All right, Commander Andertol. Show us what you

got," said Harris. "And sorry about earlier. Let me owe you one."

"We hereby reinstate Commander Andertol," Trevor said.

Neil looked at him, surprised by such a quick vote of confidence, but grateful for friends ready to stand by him.

"Thanks, guys," Neil said. "I won't let you down. I promise."

Everyone scrambled to their seats, and Neil took his original position up front. He fastened himself in with a firm click.

"Where would we even go? In case you guys haven't noticed, space is freaking huge," said Waffles.

"Mars," Sam whispered coolly.

"What was that?" asked Harris from the seat behind her.

"Mars," she replied. "Their parents were on the first manned mission to Mars. They were supposed to set up a laboratory and return after a month, but NASA lost contact with them."

"That seems to be a trend with these missions," added Harris.

"I remember seeing the satellite image of their lab on Mars," Sam said. "It got wiped out in a massive dust storm. There's no way they survived. No way."

"Plus it would take months to get there," said Corinne. "Let's not forget how far away Mars really is."

Leave it to things like logic to really throw a wrench in a plan. Corinne's point was valid, though. NASA had given the Minors a year just to get there, and Neil was certain his crew didn't have enough clean space underwear for such a commitment.

"Well, we owe it to those astronauts to make sure the same thing doesn't happen to their kids. And if Finch said that ship is our only hope, then we have to find a way to get it," said Neil, aiming the nose of the craft toward Mars. "And don't worry; I can get us there in no time."

Without warning, Neil threw the ship into warp speed. The astronauts lurched backward in their seats and felt the pressure of g forces once again press down on their bodies.

"Learned some new tricks, have we?" asked JP.

"This next one's my favorite," Neil said, flipping four switches that looked like napping monkeys. The warp drive began drawing all the reserve power from the ship's remaining systems. It wasn't the double-warp drive that Lars had used, but he'd said it was the next best thing.

From below, Boris clanged on the pipes and gave a few yelps.

"Hang tight, Boris!"

It felt like a giant boot kicked the back of the ship as it effortlessly sliced through the vacuum of the galaxy. Neil stayed firm with his controls and kept the ship pointed toward the glowing red dot broadcast on radar. It crept closer and closer, and after only fifteen minutes at double-warp speed, the planet grew from the size of a pin to a big beach ball.

The *Fossil* flew closer to the red planet, nearly exhausting all its fuel. But a familiar beeping noise started up once again, gaining intensity. The *Newt* was close. And this time it wasn't the fake radar beacon for a Canadian maritime province's nudist colony.

"You can't lose them again, Andertol!" shouted Trevor. Neil maintained his speed but gently guided the ship right, locking in on the blinking dot ahead.

The Whiptail approached Mars suddenly, and Neil disengaged the double-warp drive. It felt like seven sumo wrestlers finally got up from sitting on Neil's chest. As the ship floated just outside of the planet's atmosphere, Neil looked down at the surface below. It was filled with craters and pointy rock formations, and it looked a lot like the "before" picture for an industrial-strength acne cream commercial.

Neil realized the vast difference in planets. While the view down to Earth showcased the delicate life it contained, Mars was like a red snow globe of nastiness. Swirls of dark storms and space dust clouded the tinier planet.

"The radar's showing they're on the surface," JP said, diagnosing the computer screens laid out in front of him. "I can set us on a trajectory to their location, but visibility could be limited on the way in."

"What are we waiting for, cowboy? Let's do this!" shouted Waffles. "Operation Mars Nosedive!"

On JP's signal, Neil angled the craft toward Mars below. The nose of the ship sank down, and Neil could feel the controls begin to rumble. As their speed increased, the shaking grew more violent, jostling their helmets.

Neil did his best to hang on tight to the controls as debris and clouds enveloped the shuttle. He focused on the blue flashes of lightning and the sound of rocks pelting the Whiptail.

"Almost there," said JP. Suddenly the craft broke into clearer skies, dropping beneath the layer of storm clouds. The ground, however, was much closer than expected.

"Whoa!" yelled Neil as he jerked back on the ship's controls. They began decreasing speed but were still traveling too fast.

"Deploying emergency landing gears," said Trevor, serving as copilot.

But with an explosion of space dust, the craft slammed into the red planet. The *Fossil* skidded to a halt, and Neil let out a grunt from the force. The beeping was now a mixture of the radar and the ship's emergency warnings. He looked to the left and saw the stolen ship.

It was covered in a fine rust-colored dust, but it didn't seem to be damaged, thankfully. The *Newt* looked ten times bigger than the chimp ship, and one hundred times more modern. Its angles were more contoured, and the barrels of the rear rockets fanned farther.

"Everybody okay?" Neil asked to his team.

Eleven groans confirmed they were.

As a group, the astronauts sprinted to their air lock,

shuffling into their EVA suits while getting used to the gravity on Mars. Everyone made sure to pull down the shiny sun shield attached to his or her helmet.

Swinging the air lock door open to Mars, the group stormed out into the unknown.

Neil looked back at the *Fossil* to see that its left wing bent at an entirely new angle.

Neil and company trudged over craggy terrain to find the *Newt*'s air lock door, still shut tight.

"It's smashin' time!" shouted Waffles through his headset. He searched for a huge rock, ready to force his way inside, but the door's circular metal handle suddenly twisted and swung open.

"Please, don't hurt us!" shouted a voice. Stepping into the spooky light of Mars came two kids in space suits.

The Minors.

CHAPTER

24

"YOU HAVE THE RIGHT TO REMAIN SILENT. ANYTHING YOU talk about can and will be brought up later in conversation," hollered Biggs at the space bandits as Dale and Waffles tied them up. While it wasn't exactly a by-the-book arrest, pretty much everyone got the gist of it.

The boy and girl were silent with fear, or the need to go to the bathroom . . . Neil had a tough time deciphering the two. Either way, they didn't struggle.

"Please, we can explain," the girl said, her hair in a long blond ponytail. She had a nose that pointed up and big round ears that stuck out from her head. "My name is Kip. And this is my brother, Edmond."

She pointed to her brother, who had the rigid stance and thick neck of an athlete or soldier. Neil wondered if his nose had been broken.

"Weird names," said the person named after breakfast food.

"We're named after famous astronauts," Edmond said.

"Actually, it's great to see you," Kip confessed. "We need your help. We're not exactly sure how to fly this thing."

"Obviously," said JP.

"And did you guys really hack all of NASA's system?" asked an intrigued Harris.

"Yeah. That was the fun part," said Edmond, his voice deep like a linebacker's.

"We're just looking for our parents," said Kip.

"Clint and Elle Minor," Sam replied.

"Yeah," the boy said. "What . . . what are all of you doing up here?"

They were probably expecting a squad of elite pilots and astronauts.

"It doesn't matter who we are; what matters is that we're taking that ship and you criminals back to Earth," Trevor barked at the two strangers.

Neil was impressed by Trevor's consistency. Friend or enemy, he was a jerk to all.

"Please," the girl begged. "We know our parents are alive. They contacted us just last week."

"What do you mean?" Neil asked, frowning. The Minors had been missing for months. "I hate to say it, but I saw the memorial for your parents before we left."

"Oh, yeah," Kip said. "We've seen a few of those. Dad never looks good with a bronze face."

"Some people might think there's no chance they've survived, but we know our parents," said Edmond.

"So what are you doing?" Harris said. "You've stolen a spaceship. You think you'll just go and find your parents somewhere on Mars? Not to be a party pooper, but nobody survives out in space that long."

"Nobody but our parents. I know it sounds crazy," Edmond said. "I was watching TV last week and the channel cut out. At first it was just that static, but then, underneath it, I realized I could hear my parents' voices. They were asking me to come rescue them!"

"It's true," Kip said. "They're out here somewhere, and they figured out a way to radio home!"

But didn't NASA confirm they were lost? Weren't they considered dead a long time ago?

"Please," Edmond added. "We only want to look around here on Mars. Just help us, and then if they're not here, you can take us and the spaceship back home. I'm sure there's some reward you can claim."

The nerds circled together to discuss, placing their arms over one another's shoulders like a football team.

"Dudes, I think we head back. We get in that ship that probably doesn't smell like a barnyard and let NASA deal with everything else," said Biggs. "If an asteroid is coming, Finch can use the *Newt* for whatever he was going to use it for. Plus if I don't water one of my cactus plants in twelve hours, it's gonna die."

He had a point, or at least a half point. The best thing for all of them to do now was probably head home and gather around loved ones, such as games like Chameleon and the newest edition of *Unsupervised Science Experiment*. Families, too.

"I think we've got to try and help them," said Neil. "What if it were your parents who went missing up here?"

There was a moment of silence. It was clear the group agreed with Neil.

Slowly they walked back to the Minor twins.

"You've got a deal," said Neil. "But we only have one hour. If we don't find anything, we have to start on the trip back home."

Kip and Edmond smiled, and for the second time since leaving Earth, the crew grew in size.

CHAPTER

25

DUST SWIRLED AROUND THE CREW MEMBERS AS THEY wandered out into the desert of Mars. Their suits were quickly coated in red dirt.

"This is where they should be," said Kip. "We found the coordinates from this photo."

Kip held out the satellite image of her parents' lab to Neil.

There's no way anybody survived this.

He studied the photo of the ruined lab and dropped it to stare at the actual site in front of him. It looked even more uninhabitable than the picture promised. Sharp scraps of futuristic metal and lab supplies littered the ground, glinting in the murky sunlight.

"Let's fan out," said Neil. "Everybody start looking for clues or something. We can cover more ground this way. If their parents are alive, we have to find them."

Starting from the rubble of their parents' shelter, Kip and Edmond began frantically shouting the names of the lost astronauts. Neil knew this was all probably wishful thinking,

"No way!" yelled Dale and Waffles. Neil's heart began to race, hoping the brothers had discovered something.

The gravity was more substantial than on the moon, leaving less hang time for major jumps or potential food tosses. Neil tried to remember what Lars had said about hobbling about in low gravity.

Run like a pony or something? Lars was unlike anyone Neil had ever met, for better or for worse. Despite trying to capture him and his crew, Lars was still just a kid looking for some buddies. Having gone by the name Neanderthal for at least half of middle school, Neil knew the prickly sting of isolation.

Neil approached a small ridge and saw Waffles and Dale in an exploration rover.

It was huge, with eight all-terrain tires. One wheel was punctured, and piles of dust gathered around the vehicle.

Harris came over and nudged the machine with his foot. "We can fix that flat in no time."

The group propped up the vehicle on rocks and swapped out the faulty wheel with the spare on the back. In what seemed like seconds, they had successfully hot-wired millions of dollars in specialized NASA equipment. More miraculously, it started. The battery still worked! Waffles steered it off the ridge, landing with a crunch.

"Just like back home!" Waffles yelled.

"Well, don't break it," said Dale. "We'll drive this puppy around and keep searching. Can cover way more ground this way."

"We've got to be quick, guys. We've basically got twenty-two hours until Q-94 makes contact," Neil said.

It was Sunday afternoon, and they'd need to double-warp drive the whole way back to Earth if they wanted to get the *Newt* back in time.

"Commander, an interesting development over

here," said JP through his helmet's radio. "I think you'll want to see this."

Neil made his way to JP and stood next to him. So far, they'd barely covered much ground.

"Do you see these tracks?" JP asked, directing Neil's eyes to three flat lines pressed into the ground.

"What about them? Probably just the rover taking rock samples before it died," Neil said.

"That's what I thought, but the measurements between them are identical to the landing gear for our Whiptail," JP said. "The depth of these tracks into this top crust shows me it was a heavy craft. A Whiptail not flying but driving that way."

Neil could see the deep grooves, and he agreed it had to be the tracks of a Whiptail, or something similar. His eyes followed the ruts as far as possible, but they continued toward a mountain that looked a mile away and was barely visible.

"Well, looks like we're taking a road trip," Neil said.

CHAPTER

26

WAFFLES STEERED THROUGH THE MARS COUNTRYSIDE AND
arrived at the base of the large mountain. The tracks in
the ground continued upward.

"Got something on the starboard side," said Corinne.
Neil turned his glance the same way to see a giant roam-
ing cloud in the distance. It was a dense mix of rock and
dust, so thick Neil couldn't see through it. It looked the
size of seven tornadoes combined.

"Dust storm," shouted JP. "We need to find cover!"

The storm was headed straight toward them, already pelting the group with hail and rocks.

"Should we turn back?" asked Waffles, unsure.

"I don't think we have time!" answered Neil. He scanned the mountain. "See that little group of rocks? Let's try heading there."

Waffles steered the rover toward a pile of boulders, which looked a bit different than the remainder of the Martian landscape, but not by much.

Neil could feel the wind getting stronger as it pushed against his chest. The sun began to slip away behind clouds of dust, and Neil turned on the lights attached to his backpack. They were useless, like his family car's high beams in a snowstorm.

"Something's moving!" shouted Corinne.

Neil turned to see a hatch opening from the ground, its exterior camouflaged. Two shadowy figures crept out.

"The aliens have finally come for us!" Biggs shouted. "If they start interrogating us, nobody tell them that pizza is a thing, okay?"

The two figures that approached wore similar outfits.

"Come with us!" shouted a man's voice through his

helmet, his face hidden by a sun shield. He held out a hand in Biggs's direction. "You can trust us!"

As visibility went down to nothing, Biggs took hold. He reached back and grabbed on tightly to Corinne, who did the same for her nearest neighbor.

"Nobody let go! Follow me!" Biggs said.

The group formed a chain and cautiously followed Biggs into the hatch. Neil could hear pieces of rock collide with his helmet, and he grew worried as bigger sounds meant larger pieces.

Am I going to die with Martian mole people?

As Neil stepped down, an electronic lantern illuminated the small shelter. It was some kind of temporary structure, its walls covered with mathematic equations. The two people in grubby suits slid back their reflective sun shields.

"Mom!"

"Dad!"

"Kids!"

Kip and Edmond screamed in joy at the sight of the familiar faces. A year in space had left the astronauts looking untamed. Mr. Minor looked like a starved seventh-grade science teacher. He wore a bushy salt-and-pepper mustache that connected to a patchy beard. His wife's curly blond hair was pulled back in an unruly ponytail. Her hair took up the lower third of her helmet, like straw spread out on a floor.

She was a few inches taller than her husband, with equally yellowing teeth. It was for the best nobody could smell their breath, as outer-space dental hygiene was probably the first thing to go in a survival situation. They were both filthy, and Neil wished he knew what that kind of dirtiness felt like.

Neil and his fellow gamers watched the joyful hugs from the shocked astronauts. Biggs, Corinne, and even Trevor cried, although he tried to act like he hadn't. It was like an emotional YouTube clip, where families were at long last brought back together. Except it was happening in real life, and it didn't have a comments section.

"I knew you'd be here," said Kip, her face soaked with tears. "I knew you'd make it."

"I heard you on the TV!" said Edmond.

"We had a hunch that worked," said Mrs. Minor.

"Once we realized radio transmissions were dead and that there was insufficient fuel for a return trip to Earth, we put our noggins together," said Mr. Minor, playfully bouncing his head with his wife's. "We knew where to find this volcano, and we created an underground lab at the base to get away from these storms and continue our mission."

"And what was that?" asked Sam, enthralled. "And why the volcano?"

"Well, it's something called Q-94."

"Believe us, we know all about it," said Sam.

"We tried to get in touch, but it sounds like they figured it out, then. So you're aware that NASA's predictions were incorrect?"

"Very." The sounds of a massive dust storm raged on overhead.

"Our ship was designed to fire a special missile to harness and capture the asteroid, to be brought into our orbit to be studied," said Mrs. Minor. "But the missiles malfunctioned, and we ended up here."

"And as for the volcano, we're critically low on chemical fuel. We've got some solar panels on the ship, but they can't generate the power we need to break free of this atmosphere," Mr. Minor explained.

"We did some testing, and this volcano is past due for serious seismic activity. The way these ships are designed, and the amount of heat their armor can withstand, we can activate the thrust of the ship once we—"

"Get it flying fast enough?" answered Sam. "Believe us, we know all about that."

"So we drove the *Golden Gecko* up here, and we've been waiting patiently for the volcano to erupt, to dislodge our ship and help fire us into orbit," said Mr. Minor.

"How long have we been gone?" asked Mrs. Minor.

"You were declared lost by NASA a year ago," said Neil. "I saw the plaque dedicated to you both."

"And what about the pancakes? And the slippy seals swimming through the air?" asked Mrs. Minor, batting at the open air a few feet around her head.

"Um, repeat that back?" said Neil, unsure if these were advanced astronaut terms he would never understand.

"The lumberjacks should be here any minute. Make sure all the kittens are gift-wrapped," Mrs. Minor said, rapidly blinking her eyes and ending each sentence with a little whistling noise.

"Oh no," Sam said. "Finch had us go over something like this in that SQUID medical training."

As the crew's medical specialist, she put a hand to

the foreheads of the Minors and held her hand out, one finger pointed out.

"Follow the tip of my finger," she said to Mr. and Mrs. Minor. Sam slowly moved her finger back and forth, fixated on their pupils. She looked serious, and she took her time diagnosing her patients.

"It's just what I feared," she said solemnly. "Advanced Space Silliness. Stage two, maybe even stage three."

"What does that even mean?" asked Trevor.

"Their brains are loopy, especially Mrs. Minor's," Sam said. "A year in space all alone? The human mind isn't meant for it. We need to get them back to Earth soon, before their condition gets worse. If it goes untreated, symptoms can be irreversible."

Sam looked at Kip and Edmond, who listened with concerned faces.

"They'll be okay; we just have to get them out of here."

The news relieved the Minor children, and they once again hugged their parents tightly. Mrs. Minor looked at the group more closely, surprised.

"Why, you're just a bunch of kids," she said. "How did you even make it here?"

"Well, an old pilot hazing ritual," Neil said.

"Shuttle *Fury?* It worked?" asked Mrs. Minor. "I didn't even get past level two on that darned thing. Clint barely played two hours."

"Ha! See?" said a defensive Neil, but no one paid attention—the sounds of the storm had stopped.

Clint stood at the top of the bunker and lifted the hatch to look outside. The worst of the storm was past.

"Clint, if we're leaving, we need to get the research from the ship," Elle said as they stepped outside.

"The *Golden Gecko*," Sam said in awe. "I can't believe it actually exists."

"Oh, the old bird's in tip-top shape, too," said Clint. "Enough fuel for the warp drive back, but that's about it."

"Well, we won't even need it if you all came in a new ship."

"Well, Kip and Edmond did," said Neil. "We came in the *Fossil*."

"What?" Clint said, his face shocked. "That hunk of junk still works?"

"Complete with Boris the chimpanzee cosmonaut in the middeck," said Neil.

"He's come out of retirement? Draymond's really

shooting from the hip on this one, eh? We'll go now to the *Golden Gecko*, and we can—"

And at that moment, the desolate ground of Mars began to shake. Neil saw a slim black plume of smoke drifting up from the top of the Martian volcano.

"My cats! The volcano!" said Mr. Minor. "We've no time to spare!"

CHAPTER

27

"UH, DUDES? SHOULDN'T WE BE RUNNING AWAY FROM THE volcano?" shouted Biggs as he hoisted everyone aboard, nodding at the black smoke beginning to trickle out from the peak of the red-rock mountain. "We've got another way home, remember? Our ship isn't that far away. Or is this how I find out you're all alien robots?"

"We can't leave our ship—not yet," said Mr. Minor as Waffles drove the hot-wired rover up crumbling rocks. "The data on that ship could change life forever."

"But Finch needs the *Newt* to stop the asteroid. He said it was Earth's only chance," said Neil.

The ground shook again, and a hissing sound came from a nearby ridge. The vehicle crawled over occasional alien rock formations, slipping but regaining traction quickly. It continued climbing over the untouched mountain, nearly to the peak.

"Draymond Finch? He told you that?" asked Mr. Minor, concerned.

The rover came to a halt, as they could see a battle-tested Whiptail wedged into the small summit of the volcano. The ship was cocked at a sixty-five-degree angle, and the door to the air lock was positioned just over a smoldering crater.

The haggard astronaut briskly maneuvered to the air lock and climbed inside. Neil and the rest followed, stepping through a thin curtain of black smoke.

"Is this thing gonna blow?" asked Jason 1. "Stepping onto a volcano is probably, like, thing number one we shouldn't be doing right now."

"This eruption is a million years in the making. I'm sure it's got a few more hours in it," said Mr. Minor.

The crew walked into the cabin of the *Golden Gecko*,

which looked the same as the *Fossil*, just human sized. The whole ship had a distinct "not for chimpanzees" feel, which was a welcome change.

Grubby NASA jumpsuits hung from the chairs, and countless sealed plastic containers filled nearly every flat area.

"And what are all these plastic dealies everywhere?" said Biggs, grabbing a few of the cups, shaking them to make sure their lids were secure. "Some water conservation?"

Biggs held up a cup.

"Ah, wait one second there. I'm sorry, it was Big?" said Mr. Minor. "Mr. Big, those are samples to be brought back to Earth for research."

"Samples?" said Biggs, quickly bringing the plastic cup back down.

"Or to be refiltered and used again. It would be best if you just kept those covered," said Mr. Minor.

"We go potty in those," said Mrs. Minor, gesturing to the array of plastic receptacles strewn about the ship's cabin. Biggs gagged and immediately replaced the cups he'd taken.

"That is disgusting," said Sam. "Is this what you made us come back for?"

Mr. Minor smiled. "Yes! Plus we needed our soil samples." He shook a large plastic container filled with dirt and stones.

"Science isn't always pretty," laughed Harris. "But I'm not exactly sure what kind of science this falls under."

The ground shuddered violently. It was the volcano, and the lava inside was getting impatient for an eruption.

Neil knew he had to get the *Newt*, but lava was a danger he wanted nowhere near his crew.

"Okay, team, the plan," Neil said to the group. "Harris, can you do me a favor? You owe me one, right?"

"Sure thing, ManofNeil."

"Make sure you guys go straight to Earth, okay?"

"*Wait*, Neil, you can't leave us!" said Sam.

Neil turned to her and gave her a shrug, "Sam, we need to get the *Newt* back to Earth. I promise I'll be right behind you."

★ ★ ★

The outer door signaled it was safe to open, and Neil twisted the handle. The black smoke outside had grown thicker. Neil leaped across it to the waiting rover.

"Okay, Waffles, do I need to do anything special to hot-wire this thing?" Neil radioed back to his friends on the ship. He hopped on and adjusted the steering wheel and ignition.

"There's a clear wire and a silver one. Cross those."

Neil twisted the wires and struck them like kindling. The rover buzzed to life, and Neil looked out at the sun. It was weird thinking how it was the same burning star that kept him warm at home.

But as he gazed up at the hazy crimson sky, Neil felt vibrations furiously traveling through the metal vehicle. He turned back to see the Minors' Whiptail shuddering in the mouth of the volcano. Plumes of dark smoke soon swallowed it. Neil could feel the ground begin to shift.

"Guys, you've got to get out of here," Neil called into his radio.

There was a rumble as the ship jump-started, and he could feel the jets kick in.

Neil hopped back on the rover, doing his best to hold on with both his legs and feet as he started down the volcano, skidding over uneven rocks. He could feel the ground rumbling underneath the rubber tires, and he leaned right to avoid the splintering cracks of magma bursting up.

"Neil! Neil sch . . . it's . . . going . . . ," said Sam, her transmission crackling.

"What?" Neil shouted, looking back. The sky was drearier than normal.

"No . . . ghh . . . tsh . . . come back," said Sam through more and more static. But her last words were hauntingly clear. "I'm sorry . . ."

Neil neared the volcano's base and felt a bone-rattling blast. It sounded like a cannon fired from the bottom of a swimming pool. Neil turned to see the middle of the volcano explode in a spray of black, red, and neon orange.

Out from the chaos shot a blue streak, clearing the geyser of ash to venture out of the planet's atmosphere. Neil knew it had to be the *Golden Gecko*, and he felt good knowing his friends were safe.

CHAPTER

28

NEIL CLUTCHED THE MARS ROVER WITH EVERY OUNCE OF energy his body had left. The radio silence lingered. Neil knew the ship was probably already engaging double-warp drive, carefully using the little fuel that remained.

Neil floored the rover and headed back to the *Fossil*. He felt something deep inside his gut. Something beyond what was most likely an undigested gummy peach ring.

I'm the only person who can save the planet.

No one else could stop Q-94. As another dust storm began to sweep across the Mars landscape, Neil arrived back at the broken *Fossil*, which was completely unfit for flight. He was panting and full of adrenaline as he carefully climbed into the ship's air lock.

"Boris! Boris, I'm back!"

Neil headed to the middeck of the ship, and, after dodging a few flying bananas, helped Boris put on his chimpanzee space suit. He did his best to explain that they had to leave, using only The Universal Biggs Language, hoping Boris would understand.

Neil's watch read 14:24, and time was running out. They needed a plan. He gasped as a thought crossed his mind.

"Lars said there was an asteroid at the end of the game?" Neil said aloud. "He's, like, the only person alive that's made it that far."

Neil realized there might just be one more person capable of stopping Q-94. He and Boris grabbed three bunches of bananas and sprinted into the sleek and spacious air lock of the *Newt*, headed for the moon.

★ ★ ★

The door stamped POD 12 was locked. Neil pounded his gloved fists against the metal.

"Lars! I know you're in there!"

He kicked the bottom, and the low gravity made Neil feel like he was in a kung fu movie. Boris, at Neil's side, pounded the doorframe with his strong fists.

"I need you to teach me how to destroy the asteroid in the final level," Neil shouted into the door. He stepped back after hearing the scraping metal of the lock system. Lars opened the door a few inches, like a person inspecting a pizza delivery driver before forking over their cash.

"Why should I do that? You guys tricked me into not hanging out. You used *smells* against me," Lars screamed. "I can't sniff baked goods without thinking it's going to smell like animal feces. You know what that does to a guy?"

"Lars, you put us in a tough situation. You *were* trying to take us prisoner there for a while," Neil defended.

"Everyone's always in such a hurry to leave. I've got nobody. I'm sick of it," Lars said. "I even beat that game after you guys left."

"Shuttle Fury? Lars, I'm not going to lie. I need to know what happens," Neil said. "I'll do whatever it takes. I'll even come back and play with you. We can play online. I'll be your best friend forever."

Lars's face lit up.

"Forever? You promise?" he asked.

Maybe forever was strong language. But forever might only be a few more hours if he didn't get Lars to help him.

Neil swallowed hard.

"Promise."

Seeing full glasses of space punch just sitting out, Boris somersaulted into Lars's house. He gave a playful squeal.

"Hey there, buddy!" Lars exclaimed.

"Or . . . ," Neil said, a plan brewing. "I don't think Boris here will get along with my pet ostrich. How would you like a roommate and new space Ping-Pong partner?"

"Really?"

"He's been retired in Florida for years; he'll fit right in at your nudist colony," Neil said. "Just treat him well. He's my friend."

"Wow, thanks, Neil," Lars said.

"And the game?"

"Oh right," Lars replied. "Here's what you do. . . ."

★ ★ ★

Neil headed straight for the asteroid, following the coordinates mapped by Astronaut Clint Minor, clutching the controls of the *Newt*. It was the pinnacle of NASA engineering, and piloting the ship felt like controlling the future. Where the *Fossil* was clunky and smelled like moldy bananas, the *Newt* was clean and streamlined.

As Neil rocketed through deep space, his thoughts returned to his friends and the recently reunited Minor family.

At least they got to see their parents again, even if it was just for a few hours.

Neil wondered what his family was doing. He figured they were probably watching Janey kick a local youth in the shin. His welling emotions were paused by the sound of a low beeping.

Neil watched the ship's radar come to life. The blip on the screen was moving fast, and Neil steered right for it.

The asteroid came into view. Neil angled toward the rock. It was terrifying, spinning like a pitcher's curveball and the size of a small planet. He tried to match its slight curve and pace.

Neil gazed at the distant speck of Earth and realized it was like a dangling piñata, and this thing was about to tear through it. It was unlike a papier-mâché donkey, though, in that there was going to be 100 percent less candy.

"Remember what Lars said," Neil said to himself. It

felt reassuring to talk to someone, even if it was himself.

The instructions Lars provided offered Neil two separate steps for asteroid destruction. If one didn't work, he needed to move on to the next. If both didn't work, well, then it was game over. Officially.

Neil started in on Lars's first line of defense, directing the muzzle of the pulse cannon at the asteroid. It had its own separate joystick and screen in the middle of the control dashboard. If fired at its maximum energy level, it could potentially knock the asteroid off its path.

Neil powered the cannon and guided the joystick like a stuffed-animal crane game, gently tapping the black control. Below a picture of a lightning bolt was a black knob. Neil cranked it to full power and fired away, sending a crackling ball of energy toward the projectile.

He watched it collide smack-dab in the center of the asteroid, but the spiraling rock continued unfazed.

"This is like trying to stop an elephant with confetti!" Neil yelled as the second pulse cannon's shot exploded in a harmless blue puff. Neil did his best not to panic, but the cards seemed stacked against him.

Okay, Lars, really wish we had more than two options right now.

- -

As he watched the asteroid hurtle toward the blue dab of Earth, Neil slowly removed the glass enclosure guarding a red button. It was marked with an outline of a newt, with its lizard legs and tail.

Neil increased his speed. This was Earth's only chance of survival. He drifted to the right, speeding ahead of the asteroid's orbital path.

★ ★ ★

"Well, guys, don't know if anyone can hear me . . . ," Neil said into his radio, unsure what else to do. "But I guess this is good-bye, because this thing is probably going to explode. I just wanted to say I couldn't have hoped for a better crew."

Neil knew as commander, it was his responsibility to sacrifice himself for the team. Having earned back his friends' trust, Neil was never going to lose it again. He looked out at the glittering stars and thought of how just days ago he was Guerilla IMAXing in a planetarium.

Send a message for everyone on the Reboot Spotlight. You might as well just do it. Even if it doesn't make it, they'll hear you . . . somehow.

Neil imagined himself tapping in the IP address for Reboot Robiski's gaming site and pretended that he was filming a video of himself.

"Riley, you're the best swineherd there is," Neil stammered. "JP, Jasons, Corinne, I can't wait to hear about your next adventures. Dale and Waffles, thanks for showing me how to hot-wire something. That was a big bucket list item, so thanks."

Neil's lip began to quiver as his eyes began to fuzz with tears. In space, however, they didn't simply roll down his cheek. He had to wait for them to well up and then bead away from his eyeballs. It was all pretty scientific and annoying.

"Trevor, good luck on fencing or whatever. I hope you stab just a ton of other kids." Neil sniffled, his helmet restricting snot-to-sleeve rubbing. "Harris, I'm still glad you didn't get put in prison or anything. I can't wait to hear about Feather Duster 3."

"Biggs," Neil said, and then made a few swooping hand gestures, taking a guess at what *brothers forever* might look like in The Universal Biggs Language.

"And Sam . . ."

Neil realized maybe things were weird with Sam, because maybe they were something different than just friends. And that was okay.

- -

"Sam, you'd hate the constellations from up here. You can't tell what anything is," Neil said, sniffling as his nose ran a bit. "I'll . . . talk to you later."

With a long exhale, Neil spun his ship around to directly face the asteroid. He initiated the thrusters of his rocket, using all the fuel left in his reserve tank for a double-warp-speed-plus-fuel-drain assault. Alarms rang out as Neil headed straight for the behemoth flying rock, his thumb resting on the grooved red button.

CHAPTER

29

SAM WALKED THROUGH MATTED BROWN GRASS TO THE edge of a two-lane highway. The *Golden Gecko* was stuck in a watery marsh.

The once-elite Whiptail was now going nowhere.

Fortunately, Astronaut Clint Minor had been able to guide them back within a few miles of the NASA base on Florida's coastline.

Sam knew they had to warn everyone of the impending annihilation.

"Come on . . . somebody drive by," Sam said nervously. Her insides felt twisted.

She knew any asteroid that was able to destroy Earth would stay a secret. Everyone would keep living like a normal day.

It may not be NASA policy, but honesty is a Sam Gonzales policy. We've got to do something.

She put a hand over her eyes and squinted at the sky. Where was Neil? He should've been following just behind in the *Newt*. She hoped he hadn't done anything stupid.

Sam heard the rumble of a diesel engine. A huge black bus rolled over a nearby hill, shimmering in the heat. Sam waved both her hands frantically, signaling for the vehicle to pull over to the side of the road. The engine whirred as the driver downshifted, screeching to a halt in the middle of the swampland road. Sam's friends cheered.

Neil, I hope you're landing somewhere near NASA. We don't have time to wait.

"Where are you coming from?" asked the bus driver.

"Eh, costume party."

"In September?"

"My cousins, they, ah, graduated. From Space Camp," said Sam. "Listen, it's a long, long story. Where are *you* coming from?"

"Well, this is the bus for the baseball team," the driver said. "The Tallahassee Tough Guys. Big game today—World Series game one. They're playin' the Houston Howler Monkeys, and the president's throwing out the first pitch. Game's supposed to be broadcast to a billion people. We're headed to the stadium now; you need a lift?"

"As a matter of fact, I do," she said. "And do you have any extra room for my friends?"

"I thought you said they were your cousins?"

"Cousin friends. Why do they have to be different, you know?" said Sam as she waved her crew over to the bus. They piled in, and the driver began looking distressed as sixteen people in space suits crammed in.

"Thanks so much for the ride. Graduation day is a big deal," Sam said.

She turned to Mrs. Minor, who was near the driver as the bus lurched into gear. "Right, Aunt M?"

"Oh, we love graduating things. I'll give you directions on where we're going," she said. "Just take your next left and head north. Then a right at the giant cactus—it'll be singing; you can't miss it."

★ ★ ★

After only seven wrong turns and convincing the driver to ram a government-protected gate, the bus skidded to a halt. They were in front of the same NASA hangar they'd left from. A pudgy guard from a security post at the end of the driveway raced toward them, stepping over pieces of the shattered gate.

"Good luck on the sporting match, fellows!" said Riley, who was the last of the astronauts to skip down the bus's stairs. "Give the Howler Monkeys the comeuppance they deserve!"

The Minor family rushed into the NASA base.

"Draymond?" shouted Mr. Minor, his voice echoing as he entered the empty hangar.

"Hello? Anybody?" Sam yelled.

"I don't see him," gasped Dale after darting through the building's astronaut memorial hallway. "Want me to check outside? Think he's in the SQUID?"

"Hello? Who's there?" came a man's baritone voice.

It was Finch, walking through the hangar's double doors. He looked a mess, with bags under his eyes and wearing a wrinkled suit. He'd undone the first few buttons of his shirt, which was now untucked. He looked like a zombie version of himself. Behind him was Yuri, who apparently never left the base from earlier.

"Commander!" shouted Biggs, who made a "spirit fingers" motion with one hand while circling a four-legged hand animal with the other.

"We'd been following you all, but tech has been malfunctioning. How'd you all get back here?" he said, baffled to see the kids he sent to space earlier in the weekend. "No matter how you got back, I'm just glad to see you." But as he locked eyes with Clint and Elle Minor, his jaw dropped.

"Hi, Draymond," said Mr. Minor, his face warming with a smile. "It's good to see you."

"No, it can't be," Finch said, tears welling in his eyes. "I searched for you for months. You're missing!"

The unkempt astronaut giggled, scratching his brambly comb-over.

"What was that you used to tell us? Question everything?" Mr. Minor said. "Seems like Kip and Edmond have some explaining to do."

- -

"We have some memorials to take down," said Finch. "But first, Q-94. We've got a mission to finish."

"And a toboggan to fix!" added Mrs. Minor, who noodled her arms with Biggs-like hand gestures. "And our scientific pee collection to show you!" Kip and Edmond quietly approached their mother and wrangled her away by each arm.

"Wow, that's some stage-three Space Silliness." Finch's brow crinkled as he locked eyes with Mr. Minor. "Clint, it's too late. I wish our situation was different, but I've been tracking it nonstop. There's nothing we can do to stop the asteroid."

"But Neil was supposed to be right behind us in the *Newt*. We recovered it," said Sam. Neil was her best friend and the best leader she'd met; he wouldn't let her down.

"I checked radar and didn't see anything tailing you," said Finch.

She felt sick.

"But he promised . . . ," said Sam.

Sam knew there wasn't time for sadness. It was maybe too late for Neil, but she knew she had to try something. Anything was better than just waiting to get squashed.

"Well, we've got to do something!" Sam blurted.

"Well, at this point, our best bet is to hunker down in the SQUID," said Finch. "The asteroid's due to hit within hours, but we were wrong by days before. There's *literally* nothing else we can do."

"Come now, Draymond," said Mr. Minor. "Surely there's something else to be done?"

"Can an asteroid ramp off something to jump over Earth?" asked Jason 2. "There haven't been enough things ramping off other things for my tastes."

"Agreed," said Dale.

"Hear, hear!" added Riley.

"Can we at least get a broadcast out, Commander Finch?" Sam said. "If the world's about to end, people should at least be able to know. Even for a few minutes."

"But you can't just stir the entire population of Earth into a frenzy," the commander replied. "It would be madness."

"He's got a point. If I heard the world was ending, I would just run into a Dairy Queen and pour soft-serve directly into my mouth," Waffles said bluntly. "I could name at least four other dudes back home currently doing the same thing. And they don't even know about the asteroid."

- -

"I think Sam's got a point," said Harris. "Hear her out."

"Who is this?" asked Finch.

"Oh, that's Pickles," said Corinne. Dallas and a slew of NASA technicians entered the hangar, rushing past the filthy crew members.

"Commander, how do you know it would be madness? You have to give people a chance," Sam said. "Wouldn't you want to have the chance to say a few good-byes to people you love?"

He closed his eyes. His nostrils flared with a few breaths before he spoke.

"You're right," he said in a low voice. "I guess we've just got to be honest."

Sam thought about her friend Astronaut Neil Andertol.

"We have to tell people right away. Can you broadcast from here? Is there a camera?" Sam said.

"I think we may have something. Follow me," Finch said as he power walked to the hangar's exit with purpose.

"Follow that gingerbread man! He's getting away!" shouted Mrs. Minor.

Finch led Sam, her crew, and the family of astronauts

into the depths of the control center. Dallas looked tired and stressed, like Finch. It didn't seem like she had slept since the crew left on their mission.

"We used to do news broadcasts from right here," Finch said, pulling a dusty white sheet off a wood desk. A pair of clunky, ancient cameras pointed at two orange chairs behind it. "Hasn't been used in a decade, though. Maybe more."

"But we could broadcast to everybody? The whole country?" asked Sam.

"The whole world," Edmond said confidently. "Hacking this stuff is simple. Me and Kiki can get this broadcast on every satellite in existence."

"Well, let's hope the old dog's still got some juice," said Biggs as he turned on the studio lights.

Kip and Edmond swarmed the computers and began clacking at the old plastic keys.

Jason 1 entered the studio's control room, which was separated by thick soundproof glass. He began punching a keypad connected to a wall of TVs.

Dale and Waffles flipped bulky metal switches attached to the two cameras and toyed with their focus.

"Hey, found these under a dusty sheet," said Jason 2,

clutching two burgundy suit coats in either hand. They were emblazoned with the NASA logo and had bulky shoulder pads sewn inside.

"We've got the feed for the World Series," said Kip. "Anybody tuning in to see President Slugshoe will see our broadcast."

"You kids can really do all this?" said an impressed Finch.

"Oh, the stories we've got for you. You should ask more questions, Commander," said JP, who assumed the position of technical director. He threw on an old headset and attached the connected battery pack to his suit. "Now this is gonna be live, people. We've only got one shot at this."

Biggs and Sam plopped into the chairs behind the news desk, brushing the dust from their jackets. They slid them over their space suits, which was like putting a coat over hockey pads.

"TESTING!"

Everyone covered their ears, cringing as Jason 1's voice rang out over the speakers.

"Sorry about that. Ready for the broadcast when you are."

JP raised a hand and slowly counted down from five. As red lights atop each camera blinked on, Mrs. Minor slowly wandered into the frame. She had a pleasant smile, but her hair was still an unkempt Martian mess.

"Everyone needs to start saving their boogers," said Mrs. Minor into the camera.

"Whoa! Okay, just focus on me," said Sam. Mr. Minor escorted his wife offscreen, and Waffles zoomed the camera in toward Sam.

"Ladies and gentlemen of Earth. First off, hey. I'm Sam," she said with a half smile and wave.

"And I'm Biggs. Welcome to your five-o'clock hijacked space news."

From offscreen, Riley made the sound of a bugle.

"People of this planet we call home, there's something you need to see."

The screen cut to a shot outside. It broadcast a picture of light-blue sky, with blobs of white clouds. It was a beautiful afternoon.

"In only a few hours, Earth may . . . Earth might . . ."

Sam wasn't sure exactly what to say. But her attention was drawn to the outside camera shot. Sam watched as a ball of light appeared in the camera's lens. It grew larger, and Sam knew it was Q-94. She took a deep breath and could feel her hands tremble.

"You tried your best, Neil."

She braced herself for the asteroid to hit. But impact never happened. Sam opened her eyes. She watched the streak split, and instead it separated into tiny flares that plunged toward the ocean. It looked like fireworks.

Somehow, amazingly, Earth was safe.

The radio in her suit began to crackle to life.

"Houston? Dallas?" came a faint voice. "Sacramento? Anybody?"

"Roger," said Finch, bringing his hand to his earpiece. "Repeat your transmission?"

It sounded like Neil.

"Neil!"

"Man, is it good to hear your voice."

Sam had a radiant smile.

But then his voice was gone and static filled the studio.

CHAPTER 30

"ACTUALLY. VIEWERS. UH. THIS WILL DISCONTINUE THE emergency asteroid test. Great job, everyone," said Sam to the in-studio camera. "If this had been a real asteroid emergency, you would have heard a series of high-pitched squeaks, and my partner here would have made the universal sign for *emergency*."

Biggs looked solemnly into the camera and, placing a thumb into each nostril, waved his palms and fingers.

"But, like I said, everything is fine," Sam reassured the audience. "Go, Tallahassee Tough Guys!"

The Coast Guard patrol ship slapped across the choppy waves of the mid-Atlantic with a crew of astronauts and video gamers, heading toward a smoldering capsule.

They lifted the container onto the ship, and Finch nervously swung open the hatch door.

"Neil?" yelled Sam.

As navy-blue-clad sailors sorted through the parachute of the space capsule, they scooped Neil up to the ship's deck. Sam rushed to the entrance of the dripping metal space capsule. She looked down with worry, her chest tight.

"Did you miss me?" came Neil's voice from the darkened pod.

Neil's hands grabbed the sides of the hatch as he tried to crawl out. He was still woozy from the flight home.

"It's okay, sit down," said Finch, clutching the arm of his recruit. "Things are going to feel weird for a moment. Days even."

"I made it? Reboot got my message. Is he still here?" asked a fuzzy Neil. He was drenched in sweat.

"What? We found you in this capsule," said Sam.

"The pod. It was filling up with water," Neil

stammered. "But Reboot Robiski appeared like a dream. He threw a video controller in the water and pulled me to safety. He said he got my message."

"You just take it easy, Neil," said Sam. "I'm beginning to wonder if you're displaying stage-two Space Silliness yourself. But you did it, Neil Andertol."

"So it worked?" Neil asked enthusiastically, squinting his eyes at the sun.

"I mean, I guess it did, whatever it was," replied Finch. He patted Neil on the shoulder with his thick hand and gave him a smile.

"That button—" Neil said as he took a space blanket from Dallas.

"You mean it worked?" asked Finch, jumping into the conversation. Soldiers attended to the Minor parents as well.

"That's the top secret level of Shuttle Fury, though. How did you know what to do?"

Neil rubbed the back of his head. "Or at least I think that's what it did. I pushed it right before I was due to hit the asteroid. Faster than double-warp drive and everything."

"Just like we designed it!" said a rejoicing Dallas.

"I think whatever happened, the ship shot me off in

a one-man capsule back to home," Neil said. "The only thing I remember seeing was the asteroid colliding with the ship. But it looked like a giant food fight."

Without asking, Sam went up to Neil and gave him a hug. It was one of those ultralong, several-deep-breaths types of affairs. He looked at his friend with tired eyes, and they didn't need to say a word.

"Neil Andertol, I thought you were a goner!" shouted Biggs, disrupting the tender moment. "I worried we were gonna have to go back to Mars to find your body all shriveled up."

"Nobody's going back to Mars!" said Mr. Minor. "Don't worry."

Neil looked at the reunited Minor family.

"Thanks, Neil," said Kip, giving him a tight hug. "You don't know how much it means to have our parents back."

Neil gave a blushing nod and tried to take the compliment as best as he could.

"Neil, listen," Harris interrupted, hanging up from what seemed like an important phone call. "I'm actually going to have my helicopter pilot pick me up. But I wanted to say—"

"No worries, Harris," Neil said. "We don't need a sappy good-bye. You head off to your secret island chain."

"It's not *that* secret."

Neil laughed. "Well, even if it was a dumpy public island, I'd wanna come visit. You saved our mission, Harris. You're always part of this team."

Harris blinked a few times but kept a relaxed smile glued to his face.

"Neil, thanks," Harris said, the helicopter appearing overhead. "After what we've been through, that means a lot. You try and steal every video game in the world, you'd be surprised at how few people actually want to hang out."

Neil chuckled, and tried not to puke. His stomach was still in space, it seemed.

"But now I have eleven people I can call friends. And that means something."

Neil gave the billionaire's son a smile. He felt the same way.

"I still can't believe you pulled it off, Andertol," said Finch, putting a heavy arm around Neil's shoulder. Together they looked out at the pink afternoon sky.

"Even if you don't believe it, it still happened,"

said Neil, tugging down on the bulky space blanket enclosing him.

"I guess that's true. But I am sure of one thing," Finch said. "That you're an astronaut, Neil Andertol. A born space explorer."

CHAPTER

31

NEIL GRABBED THE HIDDEN KEY TO HIS HOUSE. HE PLUCKED IT from the ground and watched an earthworm squiggle in the print left behind. The twilight sky was a deep blue, and Neil paused to think how weird it was that he'd been out in the same sky. Neil wondered what kind of rules applied for outer-space jet lag.

Despite awful things like villains, the sound of Styrofoam rubbing together, and little sisters, Earth was a pretty cool place. It was like its very own spaceship, floating in the huge sea of outer space. Plus it had video games and TV and stuff.

Neil turned the key and pushed the door open with a creak.

"Hello? Guys?" he shouted. "Is there a new karate champion in the house?"

But the house was quiet, the only noise coming from the gentle hum of the refrigerator.

From the backyard, though, Neil heard a familiar squawk.

"Oh, crap. Regina!" Neil yelled, having completely forgotten about her. He raced out the back door. A crescendo of ostrich warbling rose out from the yard.

Doubling the normal meal amount, Neil gave her two huge scoops of pellets, and a heavy pet and fluff.

"Oh, there you are, Neil," said his mother, pushing her sunglasses to the top of her head. "Come inside. Your sister has a very cool new trophy to show you."

Relieved that life had returned to normal, Neil trotted back into the house.

"So how was the weekend? I didn't hear from you the whole time! You must've really gotten along with the sitter," said Neil's mother, giving him a kiss on his head as he attempted to squirm away.

Uh-oh. What happened to the babysitter?

"It was pretty great. Went by fast," Neil answered, wondering how soon he'd be able to slip upstairs to give Shuttle Fury another try. He wanted to know how it compared to the real deal.

"Out of this world," said Mrs. Andertol, grabbing the remote for the small television on the kitchen countertop.

Neil froze, and his jaw hung slightly open.

"Uh, what?"

"Out of this world, you know. Out of sight," she said. "Far-out. Is that a thing that people still say?"

"Oh," Neil said, laughing at the thought that his parents would ever discover his military and space-exploring past. "I don't think so. Where's Janey?"

"Oh, she's in her room. No pizza for her tonight, and she has to write a five-page letter."

"To whom?"

"The tournament judge she karate-chopped in the back of the knee."

"Whoa, really?"

"He had it coming!" yelled Neil's little sister from upstairs.

- -

"It was a rule infraction, young lady. Now you have to deal with it!"

Neil laughed. It was good to be home. He began to leave the kitchen.

"Before you disappear, go help unload the groceries, please," Neil's mother ordered. "Tonight we're having kale salad and a pizza for you. I swear we ate nothing but ravioli this whole weekend."

Neil headed for the garage, then heard his mother gasp. It sounded bad. He spun around to see the whole Minor family on cable news, waving proudly from NASA.

"They made it back!" Mrs. Andertol shrieked.

Neil grinned as he watched Elle and Clint stoop down to receive blue-ribbon awards—the Medal of Unwavering Honor. Neil remembered standing in the museum/buffet just days before, wanting more than anything to receive such an honor.

I'd rather help two kids find their parents and save the world than get a medal any day.

Neil went to the garage. The family utility wagon had a small mountain of white grocery bags waiting for him. He grabbed the thin plastic handles of five white bags.

"Package for you, Mr. Andertol," said a deep, familiar

voice. Neil turned around to see Jones in the driveway, standing behind the car.

"Major General, sir," Neil said, saluting Jones. Jones handed Neil an envelope, LEVEL TWELVE inked in black across it. Neil held it with both hands and began to imagine the possible adventures it could contain.

This time, whatever it is, I'm actually playing the whole thing.

"Open it," said Jones.

Neil pulled out a case. It was black felt, and not a video game, like he'd expected. Neil opened the square box, which creaked like a tiny, startled frog. Inside was a medal, like the kind dangling around the necks of Clint and Elle Minor.

In engraved letters it read ASTRONAUT NEIL ANDERTOL.

Neil smiled and looked at Jones. The two shared a salute as the garage door slowly rolled shut.

ACKNOWLEDGMENTS

I'd like to offer my deepest gratitude to my editors, the amazing and insightful Hayley Wagreich and Catherine Wallace. I also wish to thank the team at Alloy, including Josh Bank, Sara Shandler, and Les Morgenstein. And thanks to the art department at HarperCollins—Alison Klapthor, Alison Donalty, and Barbara Fitzsimmons—for making sure the nerds have a cover that's as fun as they are.

To Meryl, my family, and my friends: this truly would not have been possible without your support. My appreciation for you all is unending.

DON'T MISS THE FIRST
NERDY ADVENTURE!

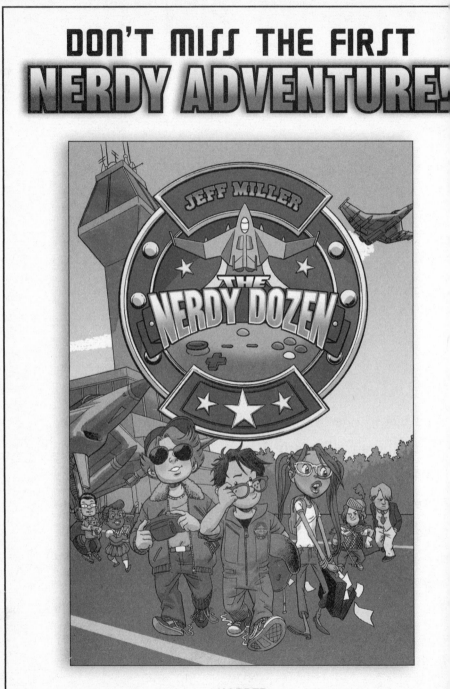